Stories in the Old Style

Stories in the Old Style

Al Sim

Press 53
Winston-Salem, North Carolina

Press 53
PO Box 30314
Winston-Salem, NC 27130

First Edition

This book is a complete work of fiction. All names, characters, places and incidents are products of the author's imagination. Any resemblances to actual events, places or persons, living or dead, are coincidental.

Cover design by Kevin Watson & Al Sim
Cover art by Geoffrey Atkin

Grateful acknowledgment is made to the following publications in which these stories first appeared:

Antietam Review, "The Waving Man"
Chiricú, "No Mix"
Crab Creek Review, "Two Head Gone"
Devil Blossoms, "The Bitter Taste"
Fourteen Hills, "The Bully Bleeder"
Glimmer Train, "Get the Can"
Lynx Eye, "Chuy's Truck"
New Millennium Writings, "Nick the Greek"
North Atlantic Review, "The Bootlegger's Toes"
Portland Magazine, "Fetch"
Projected Letters, "La Estupidez de Cosas"
Red Cedar Review, "Fear of Politics"
Rockhurst Review, "Hungry Winter"
Saint Ann's Review, "The Ugly Wife"
Talking River Review, "Last Round Joey Two Bits"
The Literary Review, "The Freedom Pig"
The Raven Chronicles, "Bargains and Dust"
Thin Air, "Reefer Diamond"

Printed in the United States of America

ISBN 0-9772283-3-9

Acknowledgments

Kurt Vonnegut warned writers to not "open a window and make love to the world." His advice was to choose one person—someone you know and admire and respect, someone who shares your sensibilities, and perhaps most importantly, someone you want to impress—and write for that one person alone. For me, that person is my wife Jill. I wrote every one of these stories for her. These stories would not exist without her. Her good opinion means everything to me, and I am still elated every time that I win it.

This book, the stories as they are collected here, the object you hold in your hands, would not exist without Kevin Watson. He is a gifted editor, an intrepid publisher, and a true friend. He trusts you to know your own work best, but does not extend that trust into indulgence. He manages the neat trick of sympathetic objectivity, the greatest service an editor can provide—and a rare and valuable quality in any human being.

I'd like to mention friends and family who have been supportive and encouraging, but I'm afraid I'll forget a name or two and bruise some feelings. So I will mention just the most zealous and let her represent them all. My mother-in-law, Carol Peckham, has been a devoted and avid reader, and a vocal enthusiast. She has always made me feel that I was accomplishing something with my work, even when reason argued that I was not.

And I would like to thank all of the editors who accepted these stories in their original publication. Your approval has been invaluable.

Al Sim

for Jillian, my beloved

Contents

Get the Can

He was the only haole kid in sight. He was standing in the middle of a tidal channel between the lagoon and the brimless Pacific. They called it Drifter's Reef, but there was no reef out here, just restless green water. He wondered what the Japanese called it when they built the bombed-out causeway he was standing on.

The causeway was made of huge slabs of concrete, stood on edge and bolted together. Narrow gaps a few inches wide separated the slabs. These gaps were filled with water and life. Little Day-Glo fish swam in the one beneath his feet. He crouched down to get a better look at them. Mike came over and crouched down next to him.

"Pretty neat, yah?" the Japanese-Filipino boy said. "Big schools in da little cracks."

Mike wasn't short for Michael. It was short for Microphone. His father the air traffic controller named his first son after the piece of equipment that took them out of the slums of Manila. It actually said "Microphone" on the boy's birth certificate.

The haole boy thought about that while he watched the fish. *His name is Microphone.* The two boys squatted and watched the little violet and scarlet and electric orange fish swim beneath their toes.

"See da one," Mike said.

His finger stretched toward a tiny pale green fish.

"Poison. Eat it, you die fast."

The haole boy glanced at Mike's dark face to see if it was a lie. He couldn't tell. He looked back at the little fish, but it was gone.

"Why would I eat it?"

The other boy shrugged.

"Mebbe you get hungry."

Mike got to his feet and wandered off down the causeway. The haole boy watched the psychedelic schools of tiny fish for a moment longer, then rose and followed his new friend. They stood at the end of the pitted concrete roadway, where an American bomb had neatly severed it. He looked down at his feet for a moment, at the glass green water surging past, then followed Mike's gaze up to some older boys on the wooden bridge that paralleled the causeway.

One of these boys was outside the bridge railing, perched on the stub ends of the roadbed planks, holding onto the railing with his arms behind his back. He and the five boys behind him were all peering thirty feet down to the water below.

"What's he doing?" the haole boy asked.

"Gonna ride a ray," Mike said.

The haole boy had no idea what that meant. Then there was hollering above him, and the boy outside the railing let go and dropped into a dive. The other boys cheered when something happened underwater. Then they fell silent, and what seemed like minutes went by. The haole boy thought the boy underwater must surely be drowned. What seemed like more minutes passed. Just as panic started to rise in the haole boy's throat, the diver burst out of the sea forty feet away, his fist in the air, yelling victory.

"Come on," Mike said, and they went up on the bridge.

❖ ❖ ❖

The bridge was made of heavy timbers and planks treated with creosote. Traffic was almost nonexistent and slow moving. A few times a day, a rusted car or truck, ragged holes eaten into its sheet metal by the salt air, rumbled across going a few miles an hour.

The haole boy leaned on the low timber guardrail and watched the manta rays pass underneath. They were big silent slow-motion bats easing from the lagoon out into the deep water, riding the current like hawks on an updraft. He was transfixed.

One of the older boys was Connor Delima, the eldest Delima boy. It was Connor's turn outside the railing. He dove out and dropped into the water, grabbed a ray that looked eight feet wide, and disappeared when it banked down at a sharp angle.

"He betta let go," someone said.

Then they waited. And waited.

"He betta let go," someone else said.

They waited some more. The haole boy stopped breathing. Far too much time passed. The haole boy had to start breathing again.

Then Connor bobbed to the surface what looked like a quarter mile away, almost where the water started to churn as it headed into the open ocean. He yelped once and waved, then went into a crawl and made his way over to the slow water behind the remains of the causeway. A few moments later he scrambled up on the concrete and put his fist in the air.

"He shoulda let go," someone said. "He coulda drown out dere."

Joseph, the second-oldest Delima boy, went down to meet his brother. The others waited. The haole boy tapped Mike on the shoulder.

"You ever do that?" he said.

Mike shook his head.

"Not old enough yet. Not allowed till you thirteen."

Mike turned back to watch the Delima boys approaching each other along the shore.

"Older boys won't let you till you old enough," Mike said. "Keeps it safe."

Nothing about it seemed safe to the haole boy, and he liked that. He looked down into the water and imagined what it would feel like to ride a big black manta ray, dropping from the bridge into the water, grabbing the strange flat fish, zooming out into the cool green current.

❖ ❖ ❖

He was still daydreaming when the two Delima boys came back onto the bridge.

"Any more rays?" Connor said.

A few heads shook.

"Nah," someone said.

Connor sat on the guardrail and Joseph sat next to him. A breeze came up and rustled their hair. Little wisps danced on seven dark heads and on one blond one.

"That looks like fun," the haole boy said. "I'd like to try it."

Seven dark heads turned his direction. Connor broke into a grin. His square white teeth looked like enameled tiles.

"You would, yah? How old you?"

The haole boy looked around. Only Connor was smiling.

"Ten."

Connor nodded.

"Three more years," he said, and looked away.

Mike whispered *told you* in the haole boy's ear. Connor turned back and his grin was gone.

"You ever play get da can?"

The haole boy hesitated, then shook his head. He didn't know what the older boy was talking about. Connor stood up.

"Come on," he said.

❖ ❖ ❖

The younger boys followed Connor and Joseph off the bridge. The haole boy asked Mike what was going on.

"Ya gonna play get da can."

"What's that?"

"Throw a can in da wata, wait till it sink, go get it."

The haole boy's heart skipped a beat. Connor and Joseph led them out onto the causeway.

"Connor," Joseph said.

Connor stopped and turned.

"You gotta can?" Joseph said.

Connor smiled, then pointed at the water on the up-current side of the causeway, where the water slowed and pressed against the pitted concrete. He went about ten paces further and dove in. About forty seconds later he came to the surface and tossed a rusted Coke can to his brother.

The can made a rattling, crunching sound. Joseph tilted it to let the water drain and a coral pebble tumbled out. He decreased the angle to keep the other stones from following.

Connor got back up on the concrete and walked over to the haole boy.

"Here da rules. I toss da can in da wata, over here where current's not so bad. When bubbles stop, you go get it. Easy, yah?"

The haole boy looked at the water.

"How deep is it?"

Connor shrugged.

"Not too deep. Thirty, forty feet."

Joseph stepped over and stood next to the haole boy.

"It's about twenty-five feet, maybe a little more," Joseph said. "Connor just wants to scare you."

The haole boy noticed that Joseph spoke in complete sentences and without a pidgin accent. He looked up and studied's Joseph face. The non-haole kids spoke proper English when they wanted to make him feel better. He almost smiled, then looked back down at the water.

Twenty-five feet, maybe more. Twice as deep as the deepest swimming pool he had ever been in. And full of living things he had never seen the likes of. And with a steady current pushing against the causeway, sucking every loose thing out into the ocean.

"Sure," he said. "That's simple."

Connor grinned at him again, flashed his little rows of bright white squares.

"Why do you wait till the bubbles stop?" the haole boy asked.

"So you can't follow 'em down," Joseph answered.

"Why don't you fill the can with water so it doesn't leave any bubbles?"

Joseph looked at his brother.

"This one thinksa ever'thin'," he said.

Connor grinned again. Joseph explained.

"With water in it, the can goes straight down. It's too easy to find. Air makes it skip around a little, because it floats some. It doesn't go straight down."

The haole boy nodded.

"Sure," he said. "Makes sense."

He stared into the water.

"You want me to go first?" Joseph asked.

The haole boy glanced up at him, then looked at Connor's blank face. He turned back to Joseph.

"No," he said.

Joseph patted the haole boy's shoulder, then handed the soda can to Connor. Connor put his thumb over the hole and shook the can like a maraca for a second or two. Then he spoke to the haole boy.

"When I say go, okay?"

The haole boy was staring into the water again.

"Okay?" Connor repeated.

The haole boy snapped his head around.

"Sure," he said.

Connor flipped the Coke can into the water. The haole boy moved to the edge of the concrete and stood in a slight crouch. Eight boys waited in silence, eyes on the small stream of bubbles. They fizzled and stopped. A moment passed.

"Go," Connor said.

❖ ❖ ❖

The haole boy jumped almost straight up, and dove almost straight down. He went about five feet under without a stroke. Down below him, the can had tilted slightly, and a last few bubbles had slipped out. He saw the little flashes of silver emerge from the opaque layer below and he swam toward them.

The water grew colder and greener and his chest felt heavy. He saw dark forms swimming away from him, nothing too big, probably the outer fringes of a school of mullet. He couldn't help hoping that a ray would come along and he could grab a ride.

Another silver flash, below and a little to his left, and he changed course. Then he could see a glimpse of red, and he swam toward that. He lost it in the murk, but kept going and it emerged again.

He found the can standing upright on a seaweed-covered block of concrete from the bombed-out causeway. The concrete chunk was about the size and shape of a steamer trunk. The seaweed billowed in the current, tendrils about three feet long rising up around the can. His heart throbbed as he swam close and reached in among the waving fronds, clutched the can, and turned to the surface.

He paused when he saw it, high above him, a rippling greenish-silver ceiling. It looked dangerous and angry and too far away, too far to go. He watched it shimmer and undulate like spilled mercury, and somehow it came closer and grew softer.

He wondered if Mike and Joseph were worried he would drown. Part of him wanted to stay down there, watching the surface shimmer and ripple, and wait to see how long it would take before someone came in after him.

He let a few bubbles slide out of his mouth and watched them wobble and rise. Then he gave a sharp kick and let the big bubble in his chest carry him upward. The rusted can felt perfect in his tight little hand.

The Bootlegger's Toes

1

He stopped on the bank of Vickers Creek, hands on his knees, and gasped for his breath. The cold air was tart in his mouth and hard on his lungs. He swore quietly, then put a boot through the thin ice and slogged out into the stream. When the icy water reached his groin, it clamped onto his genitals like a frigid claw, and he popped up out of the water and stifled a yell. When he landed, he had to struggle for his footing.

He swore to himself again, then started against the current toward brambles that hung low over the water. He stopped and turned when the hounds crested the ridge. Their echoes faded in the valley behind them and each dog's voice became louder and more distinct. He turned back and struggled against the flowing water.

Under the brambles, the channel was narrow and deep. The water was up to his arm pits and the briars cut at his face and hands. He pushed on for ten more yards, into the middle of the thicket. He stopped when he heard the hounds burst out of the woods behind him and tumble down the embankment. He stood still in the clear cold water, lowered himself till it ran over his upper lip, and tried his desperate best to not make a sound.

The hounds made fuss and racket till the Federal men arrived, then quieted down and went back to work. He could hear the men's low voices and the yelps and commotion of the dogs as they spread out over the steep rocky bank. He knew the men had lights but couldn't see any shining through the brush. *That's good*, he thought, *I'm well back, buried.*

After a few moments, the men gathered together and talked things over. No wasted words and none of them intelligible. *Now they'll split up*, he thought, *half'll go upstream and half'll go down.* A few seconds later he heard footsteps and dogs and cursing above him as the upstream pack made its way along the thorny edge of the gully leading to Hernaut Road.

He waited until he hadn't heard a sound in at least three minutes, then started moving upstream again. He almost fell several times when his numbed feet didn't do quite what he wanted. The briars were off the water now, by three feet or more, and he could see moonlight on the smooth pool before the bridge. Then he heard them coming back, the hounds yelping, men and dogs running, and he turned back into the thorns. His right ear felt like it was torn off, and drops of blood froze on his earlobe.

❖ ❖ ❖

He woke up when the water came into his nostrils. He tried to get a footing but his legs seemed to fade into nothing, his feet were gone. He found that he was floating and let the water carry him for a while, back the direction he had come. Then he had a sudden fear that the lawmen might wait for him where they had lost his trail. He got his feet working and moved upstream toward the bridge.

He came out of the thicket and there was light overhead. It was dawn. He waded slowly out of the water and made his way along the bank on the flat rocks at the stream's edge. He climbed up alongside the bridge and stopped just short of Hernaut Road, then stuck his head out and glanced both directions. Nothing. No one.

He turned toward home. His outer clothes froze while his inner clothes grew steamy. His feet started to burn and he hobbled. He wiped his ear and the frozen blood thawed on his hand. He was startled to see it when he glanced down to put his sodden gloves back on.

His wife was waiting up. He saw her hollowed eyes, knew she hadn't slept, and felt his remorse thickened with guilt. He fell into the new rocking chair next to the wood stove in the kitchen. She crouched down before him. She untied and loosened the laces of his right boot, wrestled it from his foot, and peeled off his wool sock. She grimaced when she saw his toes. Then she sent their oldest to fetch Doctor Van Syke.

❖ ❖ ❖

John Dilts woke at dusk, his nose full with the smells of beef stew and pumpkin pie. He groaned with relief and hunger, then groaned in anguish as the pain from his feet came up over him.

"Mary," he croaked.

He could hear her out in the kitchen, padding around in her worn slippers. The direction and volume of the sounds she made told him he was downstairs, in the back bedroom they used for guests and sickness. The old house was otherwise silent. John wondered where the kids were.

"Mary!" he tried again, louder this time.

The sounds in the kitchen stopped and her footsteps padded toward him. She appeared in the doorway, silhouetted in the frame by the light coming down the hall. The room he lay in was dim. Dusk light seeped in under the curtains.

"What time is it?" John asked.

"Four-thirty or so."

"Where's the kids?"

"I sent 'em to Donna's. You need peace and quiet."

He nodded.

"How're ya feeling?" she asked.

"Okay, considering."

He pointed down the bed.

"How're my feet?"

She hesitated for a moment, then she moved into the room and sat on the edge of the small straight-backed cane chair next to the bed.

"You lost some toes."

He paled. He hadn't thought it that bad. *Lost some toes.*

"How many is some?" he asked.

❖ ❖ ❖

John Dilts had not previously appreciated his toes. He had mostly cursed them, for he was forever stubbing them in the dark while dressing in the morning. He had a quick step and would smash a toe pretty thoroughly. They had become scarred and gnarled ahead of their time, testy and inflexible.

Now he lay in bed and looked down at his bandages. He twitched his remaining toes and winced. It wasn't the pain he winced at, though there was plenty of that. It was the sickening sense of absence, the false feeling of movement, the shrug of little phantoms.

2

The first visitor came by the next morning, Mrs. Derby from down the road, carrying an apple pie. She looked like an apple pie herself, round and dimpled and slightly glazed. Mrs. Derby was a churchgoer, wasn't usually given to visiting bootleggers. Mary let her in, watched her carefully, measured every word and gesture. Mrs. Derby asked after John, poked her head into his sick room, then sat and talked with Mary. They chatted aimlessly for a while, then Mrs. Derby got down to it. She jerked her head toward the sick room and lowered her voice.

"Terrible thing to have happen."

Mary nodded. Mrs. Derby straightened her skirt.

"Must've been horrible."

Mary nodded again. Mrs. Derby nodded back, then shook her head and clucked a little.

"Will he be able to walk all right?"

Mary watched her impassively for a moment.

"Doctor says it's too early to tell."

Mrs. Derby nodded and frowned, then sat silent for almost half a minute.

"How many toes did he lose?"

Mary smiled and showed her out.

❖ ❖ ❖

"Your toes have become the object of speculation," Doctor Van Syke said.

He was carefully unwrapping the bandage on John's right foot. John watched for a while, waited for the doctor to say more. Mary stood in the doorway. A faint guilty look passed over her face.

"What do you mean?" John eventually asked.

The doctor pulled away the last wrapping, leaned over the foot and sniffed. He was an older man with silver gray hair. John looked at the top of his head, noticed the small bald spot in the back.

"I mean everyone is asking me how many I took off."

John looked at Mary. His frown was almost a glare.

"How'd they find out?"

Mary shook her head.

"It's a small town," the doctor said. "You have children—"

"The children don't know," Mary interrupted.

Doctor Van Syke glanced at her, then went back to work. No one spoke for a moment or two. The only sounds came from the doctor's movements.

"There are few secrets in a small town," he said.

Mary nodded. John glanced at her, his face softer now, apologetic. She smiled at him. He turned his eyes away.

"What do you tell them?" John asked.

The question hung in the air. Mary glanced at John, saw he was watching the doctor.

"Tell them?" the doctor replied.

"When they ask about my toes."

Doctor Van Syke shifted his weight, examined the foot from a different angle.

"I tell 'em it's none of their damned business."

He straightened up and looked at John.

"But that won't satisfy 'em. They'll come knockin'."

He re-wrapped the right foot and began working on the left one. The right foot throbbed from all the attention and John thought to request some whiskey. He thought about it some more and decided against it.

❖ ❖ ❖

They kept coming the rest of the week, housewives and even a widow or two, asking after John's wellbeing, bringing bread and cookies and more pies, all of them hoping to wheedle a number out of his wife. But she wouldn't tell and John's feet were hidden in bandages. A few men came by to see John, but they took one look at him and lost the nerve to ask. So they would step out of the room and pester Mary instead. Mary never told her husband the one question on all those tongues, the insistent and endless *how many did he lose*? But John knew what the visitors wanted, and when his look went right through them, those with a soul felt a chill the length of their spine.

❖ ❖ ❖

"Your toes are now the object of *financial* speculation," Doctor Van Syke said.

He was working on John's right foot again. He had the bandage off and his face down low, examining the wounded flesh.

"What?" John said.

"Dick Moser's takin' bets."

John frowned, then snorted.

"Bets? On how many toes I have?"

"Hmm."

John frowned again, then shook his head.

"Not exactly," the doctor said.

"Not exactly what?"

Doctor Van Syke sat up. He looked at John over his half glasses, looked his patient in the eye and held it till John glanced away.

"On how many toes you lost. He's takin' bets on how many toes you lost. Tried to bribe me into tellin' him."

"What'd you say?"

"I told him he was a worthless drunkard and he'd better not irritate me further or I wouldn't patch him up the next time he wrecked his truck."

John grinned.

"Thanks."

The doctor allowed a tight smile.

"No need. It was entirely my pleasure."

He went back to work. John tried to stay calm, but he kept imagining his hard fist smashing into ugly Dick Moser's big crooked nose.

3

Six weeks were gone since John Dilts lost his toes. He was up and about, with the help of a thick oak cane that had belonged to Mary's grandfather. He needed some things, so he had his oldest drive him into Lime Town. His feet still hurt too much to work the pedals of the truck.

He would go see Dick Moser, the only shopkeeper in Lime. Moser's closest competitor was an hour drive away, much too far for the few things John needed. Moser's General Store was on Main Street, in the middle of the middle block. John told his son to stay with the car, then he went inside and found a clutch of men standing around the shopkeeper. He glanced at them, saw they were the town's most worthless elements. They stopped talking when they saw John.

"Well if ain't Bootlegger Dilts," Moser said.

"Don't call me that, Moser. It's a risk to a man's liberty."

"Well that's what you is, ain't it?"

John looked past him, stared at the clock behind the cash register.

"I'm not in the trade. Anyone says I am is a liar."

Moser curled his lip.

"So you ain't bootleggin' no more? Ain't got enough toes for the job?"

The assembly snickered loudly. John moved past them, to the back of the store. He stood in front of the nails and waited for his blood to cool. He took a burlap bag of tenpenny nails, then made his way around the store, gathering what he needed, using his cane hand to tuck things into the crook of his other arm.

When he returned to the counter, Moser said:

"How many'd you lose, Dilts? There's some real money ridin' on it."

Another hiss of snickering. John put the items he carried on the counter. He looked down, shifted his weight to the other foot, passed his cane to the other hand. Then he looked up, stared at Moser, burnt holes into the other man's skull.

"Why do you want to quantify my suffering?" he said hotly.

Dick Moser jerked his head back and frowned. The room was silent, the front door banged shut, then it was silent again. Moser snorted, looked around at his cronies, swallowed noticeably. His scrabbly Adam's apple lurched up and down.

"It ain't your sufferin' we're interested in, John. It's yer damn toes."

There was laughter like a bunch of cackling geese. John waited till they were done.

"Give me four boxes of twelve gauge shells," he said.

The shopkeeper turned to a cabinet behind him, found the shotgun shells, turned back to the counter.

"That it, Dilts?"

John nodded. Moser rang up the sale, money changed hands. John put his change away, then stood and stared at the shopkeeper. The conversation around him stopped.

"Dick Moser, you will never close those bets."

Moser squinted at him, took a half step back, put his hands on the counter.

"Not while yer alive, maybe."

An onlooker shifted uncomfortably, another cleared his throat.

"Not ever," John said. "I will most definitely outlive you."

The way he looked at the shopkeeper made the collected hyenas scatter. Some moved further away, others left the store altogether. Moser opened his mouth, but said nothing, just left his jaw hanging for a moment, then shut it like a box.

❖ ❖ ❖

A few days later, a shiny new black sedan pulled into the Dilts' driveway. Four men got out, self-important men in pressed suits. Mary peeked at them around a curtain, then dashed back to the bedroom. John was laying down, almost sleeping.

"John, the revenue men are here."

He felt the cold water swirling around his legs. A heavy knock came on the front door. *Moser, you bastard*, John thought.

"Let them in, Mary. There's nothing else we can do."

She disappeared. He heard the weighty voices and the solid footsteps. Mary reappeared, with the Feds behind her. They filed in and stood at the foot of his bed.

"John Dilts?" the biggest one said.

John nodded. The big man sighed noisily.

"We got a report you been smugglin' Canadian whiskey."

John didn't say anything.

"What's wrong with yer feet?"

"Frostbite."

"Oh really? Now how did that happen."

John glanced at the big man in the stiff suit, then looked at his feet.

"One of our cows was stuck in a creek. I spent too much time getting her out."

The big man sighed again.

"Sure. Sure you did. How bad you got it, the frostbite?"

John seemed to ponder the question, hesitated with his answer.

"I lost some toes."

"You lost some toes. Now how many would that be? How many toes you lose."

John stared at a spot on the big man's forehead.

"That's between a man, his wife, and his doctor."

"What?"

"He's not gonna tell you, chief."

It was one of the other Feds, a shorter and younger one. The big man gave him a patient, paternalistic look.

"I got that, kid. The question is, why not."

"Privacy," John said.

"What?" the big man said again.

John looked at the ceiling, looked at Mary, looked back at the ceiling.

"I've got a inalienable right to my privacy."

The big man frowned.

"Well now, ain't that fancy talk for a bootleggin' farmer."

Nothing happened for a while.

"Yer really not gonna tell me."

John didn't respond.

"Okay, play it your way. But I say you gotta lotta frostbite for fishin' a cow outta some crick. We chased some joker over a hill near here, lost him at a crick. That wouldn't be you, would it."

John looked at him, did not answer.

"No. I didn' think so. An' you wouldn' know nothin' 'bout the Canadian truck carryin' Canadian whiskey parked in the woods on the other side of th' hill we didn' chase you over, would ya. Nice big load a good juice. Musta been a real loss to some 'legger."

John kept his eyes on the big man and his mouth shut. It was all so vividly clear, the truck pulling up, the driver's heavy cough and his dense French-Canadian accent, the signal light flashing on and off down the road, John's frantic scramble up and over the ridge. He heard that the driver made it back across the border on foot, a good twenty miles at least, and in the coldest January anyone could remember. The lookout got caught, but the Feds had nothing to hold him on.

John slowly shook his head. The big man nodded, then the revenue men filed back out. Mary followed them to the door. While their backs were all turned, she gave them the finger.

They returned the next day with a search warrant. They didn't find a drop. John was out of the trade, and his personal supply was with Doctor Van Syke. They went about the search half-heartedly, as if they knew it was a waste of time. John kept wishing they'd just leave. Eventually, they did.

❖ ❖ ❖

Five months passed. The summer was hot and dry. Corn withered in the fields and grapes turned to raisins right on the vine.

In the last week of August, when the heat was finally beginning to ebb, Dick Moser got drunk yet again and crashed his truck one last time. Stephen Bestlow saw him come through Hopper's Gap almost on two wheels, straighten up for twenty yards or so, then fly out of control and smack into the corner of Daniel Smith's barn. The barn wasn't going anywhere, and Moser's truck folded like a rotten squash.

Everyone knew that Dick Moser was a bad drunk and a worse driver, but they couldn't help talking about what John Dilts had said, his heated prediction that he would outlive the shopkeeper. They talked, and their anxiety grew, and they cast long eyes on the Dilts family.

Then Mrs. Derby came back from visiting her sister in Camden, and finally told what she had seen that March past, those two days when the suited men in the shiny black car came up her road and everyone knew the only place past hers was the Dilts', and it just days after Dick and John squared off in town.

She tried not to gossip, Mrs. Derby, and had seen fit to keep her mouth shut all these months, but now, why, with what had happened...

Some even said that John Dilts sold Dick Moser the whiskey that killed him, that it was spiked. Most people felt that was going too far, that Moser wasn't stupid enough to buy whiskey from a man he was feuding with. But they all gave John Dilts a wide berth, and they gave him a new respect.

4

The world moved, in time, space, and history. Prohibition was repealed. The Great Depression and the Dust Bowl came and went. Despite all predictions to the contrary, another World War was fought—and in it, millions died in ghastly new ways previously unimagined, civilians and soldiers alike slaughtered with modern efficiency. Among them were many sons of Lime Town, and even a couple daughters.

You would think people would have forgot all about John Dilts' toes. But when he hobbled through Lime, someone always stared at his feet. When they thought he didn't see, they would point and whisper. And to his back they always called him *Boot*-legger Dilts, in reference to boots less full.

He pretended to ignore them, but he saw and he heard and he knew. *No matter,* he thought, *I have prospered.* And that he had. He owned a good slice of Hellegers Valley and everyone knew he was the best farmer in the county. He grew corn and apples and pumpkins and winter wheat and anything he could persuade the rich rocky ground to yield up.

John Dilts died as he wanted to, an old man in his own bed, surrounded by his family and his land.

The passing of Bootlegger Dilts was an event in Lime Town. He was respected, even feared, but mostly everyone still wanted to know how many toes he had lost. He died in the middle of a frozen January, fifty years to the day after his last night "in the business," that frozen night when he disappeared into Vickers Creek. People noticed the anniversary and talked.

❖ ❖ ❖

Matthew Dilts feigned disinterest in all the talk of his grandfather—but he listened closely.

It was commonly agreed that Matthew was more like the patriarch than any of Bootlegger Dilts' other descendants. He looked like John Dilts and he talked like him—which means he didn't talk much. And he had the same steely dignity, even as a boy. Old Mildred Hobbs said that Matthew Dilts was the very image of his grandfather as a young man. And Mildred had cause to know, for she had fancied John Dilts at that age, and had made close study of him.

Matthew was fifteen years old when his grandfather died. It affected him deeply, but no one knew. The boy held it close, like he did everything else.

❖ ❖ ❖

It was ten degrees below zero on the night that Matthew snuck into the funeral home. He used a pen light to find the basement door, then crept down the icy stone stairs. The hairs on his neck came up and wouldn't go down, but he never slowed, and he never hurried.

The embalming room was deep in the tomb-like basement. When he reached the bottom of the stairs, he stopped and used the penlight to find his object.

Then he made his way carefully across the concrete floor, toward the lone surgical gurney in the far corner of the room. His eyes never left it.

He stopped at the gurney's side. He looked down at the shrouded form, took in the contours that revealed a man's final rest. Then he stepped to the foot end of the gurney, held the pen light in his mouth, and used both hands to roll back the sheet. His hands shook ever so slightly.

How many, you ask.

Fear of Politics

They were sitting in the car when the rain started. Big fat drops fell in heavy clusters, then steady medium drops slanted in from the south. They sat and watched the pavement turn dark.

The man in the driver's seat was in his early thirties. He was short and trim, wore black glasses and had a neatly cropped beard. His name was Jack MacInnis. A stringy twelve-year-old boy sat next to MacInnis on the bench seat of the old sedan. The boy wore tortoiseshell glasses and bell bottoms and his straight brown hair almost touched his shoulders. His name was David Newhouse.

"That's the only luck we've had all afternoon," MacInnis said.

David looked at him.

"What do you mean?"

"At least it didn't start raining while we were out knocking on doors."

"But we're going back out."

MacInnis watched the rain and nodded.

"Maybe it'll stop by then," he said.

He started the car, drove up a hill and down the other side, made a left and parked along the curb. In that brief interval, the rain stopped.

"See?" MacInnis said, with a pale smile.

David looked and nodded. He had hoped it would pour and force them to stop. They got out of the car and went to the first house on the block, went slowly up its cracked cement walkway. The grass was bare in spots and brown in other places and the evergreen shrubs were starting to go wild.

MacInnis rang the bell. He hung his head while he waited and David wondered if he was praying. He knew MacInnis believed in God, which made him a traditionalist at the Unitarian Universalist fellowship they attended. David's older sister called it "the liberal coffee klatch," and in her definitive opinion, the coffee wasn't any good.

The door was answered by a towering elderly woman wearing a floor-length navy blue dress. Her hair was in curlers bunched tight around her head. She glowered down at them.

"Can I help you?" she sneered.

MacInnis started talking and when he said "Senator McGovern," the woman waved them off and slammed the door. She yelled something unintelligible from behind it. When they were out on the sidewalk, she swung the door open again.

"Communists!" she bellowed.

MacInnis stopped short and David almost bumped into him. The old woman shook a fist at them, then slammed the door again. A dog barked in the neighbor's house, then it was quiet.

❖ ❖ ❖

The political life of David Newhouse started in front of the family television set. He wandered into their living room one evening and the screen was filled by the head and shoulders of a man who was sweating like his shoes were on fire. The man squinted his shifty eyes and David thought that this must surely be a criminal.

"Who *is* that?" he asked.

"The president," his father answered.

"*That's* Nixon?"

"Yup."

David turned to look at his father. They were sitting next to each other on a worn out green sleeper sofa. The apartment smelled of frying potatoes and cigarettes. He could hear his mother mumbling to herself out in the tiny kitchen. He couldn't tell what his father was thinking. His eyes went back to the TV set.

"He looks evil."

"He *is* evil."

"What're we gonna do?"

"Vote Democrat."

The camera went tight on Nixon's face, crept in on the long sloping nose and the slashing eyebrows. And the sweat, all that sweat. How could you believe anything from anyone who sweated like that?

David had a teacher who sweated, a big red-faced ex-priest who taught geography. David thought about the line of sweat that always went across the teacher's forehead, the pack of Marlboro's always in his top pocket, always a dark short-sleeved shirt that didn't hide the sweat stains. The teacher had made vague statements that hinted at socialist tendencies, an unpopular stance in their conservative town. David distrusted him, but the other kids hated and feared him. The class ran like a machine.

The last time David had the ex-priest's class, he stepped out into the hallway and was stopped by a boy he knew only by sight, a football player. The football player flicked David's long hair with a middle finger. "Boy or girl," the football player said and didn't wait around for an answer.

David looked at his father again.

"I *can't* vote Democrat," he said. "I'm just a kid."

❖ ❖ ❖

They started up the stone walk that led to the next house and the dog that lived there resumed barking. The big German shepherd watched them from a window next to the front door, its broad paws up on the sill and its massive head up close to the glass. David caught the dog's eye and it growled and lunged and banged against the window. David and MacInnis jumped back.

The dog abruptly stopped barking. MacInnis took a slow step forward and rang the bell. The dog snarled and looked ready to lunge again, then a deep voice boomed from the bowels of the house.

"Maaa-*jor!*" the voice said.

The dog disappeared from the window. Sharp footsteps came from inside. An ugly man in a dark suit opened the door. Major was pacing behind him, nails clicking on the hardwood.

"What're ya selling?" the man said.

David and MacInnis stared at him.

"Out with it. You got ten seconds."

"We're going door-to-door representing Senator McGovern—"

"You people should all be rounded up and shot."

He scowled at the long-haired David.

"I can't tell if you're a boy or a girl."

"It doesn't matter till mating season," David blurted.

The ugly man in the dark suit slammed the door.

❖ ❖ ❖

Ten more houses. Another attack dog that barked and snarled from behind a window. More people who yelled and slammed doors. One old man who examined them with quiet contempt and slowly closed his door while MacInnis was still talking. No one heard Jack MacInnis out. They were called commies and pinkos and degenerates and hippies.

"One last house," MacInnis said, "then we call this fiasco a day."

The last house sat farther back from the street than its neighbors. It was a ranch house built on a gentle slope, with a curving driveway and a curving cement walk. They wound their way up the walk and MacInnis rapped on the sheet metal bottom half of the screen door. Behind it a paneled wood door stood open and the muffled sound of a radio announcer reading the news came floating out.

They waited. The announcer's voice stopped and classical music followed. MacInnis rapped again, a little louder. Steps came from inside and an old woman appeared in the doorway, a small neat woman with glasses and white hair. They looked at her warily and she grew wary.

"Yes?" she said.

MacInnis cleared his throat.

"Good afternoon, ma'am. We're going door-to-door representing Senator McGovern."

"Well you're wasting your time here."

It was as much of an opening as he'd had all day. MacInnis leaned forward a little. His voice quavered slightly.

"Are you familiar with his views on the issues, ma'am?"

She waved her hand.

"That's not what I meant. I'm already voting for him. You're preaching to the choir."

MacInnis wavered on his feet. He grew pale. He took a deep breath.

"Are you all right?" the woman asked.

"It's been a rotten day for us," MacInnis said. "You wouldn't believe what people have said to us."

The woman shook her head.

"My neighbors?"

MacInnis and David both nodded.

"I believe it all right," she said. "A rotten bunch. I'd like to move but I can't sell my house. Had it on the market for a year. Just gave up last week. Guess I'm stuck here."

David was astonished by this confession. He had never heard an adult speak frankly about finances, not even his own parents. *If you can't sell your car, you pretend you can't find one you like better*—words from his own father's lips. He looked at MacInnis and saw the same reaction on his face.

"I'm sorry," MacInnis said.

The old woman looked puzzled.

"For me?" she said, sounding a little cross.

MacInnis hesitated for a moment.

"For all of us," he said.

His hands were shaking. David looked at the trembling hands, at the tired set of MacInnis's shoulders and the weary expression on his face. No one said anything. The classical music seeped from the radio inside the old woman's unsellable house, muted by the intervening rooms. A car swept by, hissing along on the still-damp street.

That was when David Newhouse realized that Jack MacInnis had asked him along because no adult would go. The knowledge came with a hot stabbing sensation in his stomach. He looked again at MacInnis's shaking hands, raised his eyes to the drooped shoulders and the drawn face.

"Thank you, ma'am," MacInnis said.

She nodded slightly but said nothing. The two campaigners turned and went slowly back down the curving walk, MacInnis in the lead. Halfway to the street, David stopped and turned and looked back at the old woman. She was vague behind the screen door. She had always been vague behind it and he realized he didn't know her face, couldn't see it in his mind.

"Good luck," she called out.

Her voice was flat and disinterested. He wasn't sure how she meant it. A little chill went up his neck. He heard MacInnis turn to look at the old woman, heard the soles of the man's shoes scuff on the cement walk.

"Thank you," MacInnis called back.

She waved, so David waved too. Then he slowly turned away. When he reached the street he looked back and the door was empty. The muted music from the hidden radio was barely audible.

He hurried after MacInnis. The car was blocks away and fat raindrops peppered the concrete.

Last Round Joey Two Bits

I sat at the kitchen end of the bar and watched the old men drink. They were down at the other end, near the door. Harry on the business side and Joey Two Bits at the rail. I didn't know why we called him that. I asked Harry once and he shrugged and mumbled "who knows." Harry had no curiosity about anything whatsoever. Only bartender I ever met who never had anything to say.

Harry had a mean fat wife he hated to go home to, so he'd keep pouring as long as anyone was drinking. For the longest time that anyone was always Joey Two Bits. I spent a lot of late hours watching those two old men get plastered down at the other end of the bar. The owner had me stay till Harry locked up, for "insurance reasons." Always had to be two people in the joint at all times for "insurance reasons." I don't know if that was insurance as in insurance policy, or insurance as in I was supposed to insure that Harry and Joey didn't get too pigged and burn the place down.

Sometimes I'd go back to the kitchen and drink beer and listen to the radio and wait for Harry to come tell me he was locking up. But most nights I'd sit at the bar and listen to Joey Two Bits talk. He was telling boxing stories that night. Joey always told boxing stories when he was deep in his cups. He had his fists up and they were shaky.

"I was stinkin' up the jernt," he said. "Stinkin' it up real bad."

Joey was a boxer after the war. Don't ask me what war, I asked Harry and he said "who knows." Joey was a lousy boxer, always stinking up the joint, but he loved the game and had half a head for business, so he became a manager. Stank that up too, apparently. Got a fighter he believed in a little too much, told him not to take the fall. After that, Harry thinks he ran numbers for a while. But who knows, right?

When I knew him, Joey Two Bits was a sommelier at a fancy Italian place in midtown. First time Harry pulled that word out on me I told him to go screw himself. I asked him what Joey does and he says "sommelier," what was I supposed to think? Then Harry explains that means he's a wine expert, sort of like the maitre d' of wine. I made the mistake of asking Harry how Joey Two Bits went from being a lousy boxer kissing the mats to some sort of wine expert wearing an expensive suit. Know what he said? Right. "Who knows."

Harry was Joey Two Bits' best friend and his worst enemy. Every other drink was free and he'd keep 'em coming till Joey couldn't take 'em anymore. And

Joey was usually pretty far along when he got there, although you wouldn't know it. He'd waltz in, seeming sober as you please, all cool and class, then have a few and pass right out. One night he came in and sat on the banquette and ordered dinner and a bottle of wine. Had a glass or two and keeled right over on the banquette. We don't know how long he was passed out before the waiter noticed. Could've been a good fifteen, twenty minutes. I asked Harry why Joey drank like that. "Occupational hazard," he said. I expected him to say "who knows."

So like I was saying, Harry would fill Joey up most every night. So that night I was surprised when Harry said—

"Last round Joey Two Bits."

Joey was surprised too. I was too far away to see his face good, but I know what it looked like. I'd seen that face he made when he was embarrassed. His mouth went a little slack and his eyes, they were little and dark, got round. And then he got all polite and started feeling sorry for himself.

"Of course, Harry," Joey said.

His voice was deep. Smoked Camel no-filters, had that kind of leathery-sounding smoker's voice.

"Just a stupid old man trying the patience of vigorous youth with his sorry old stories," he said.

I remember him saying that exactly. He said things like that and they stuck in my head. Harry comes back with this—

"You're two years younger than me."

Then Joey Two Bits waves his hand my direction.

"I was referring to him," he says.

His other hand had his drink in it and some of it slopped out. He wasn't so steady. He tipped his glass up and nipped the rest off. Then he tossed a couple bills on the bar and went out the door all stiff-backed.

"Aw jeez," Harry said. "I shouldna pissed him off. Didn' hafta say it to him like that. Jeez."

It was the most Harry had said all night. He went around the bar and locked the front door after Joey. Then he went back behind the bar, picked up Joey's money, rang up the bill and pocketed his tip. Then he pretended to clean up. He walked up and down and dabbed at the bar with a wet cloth and mumbled to himself.

When he was done, we went out through the kitchen, out the back door, and Harry locked that one too. We said good night and he went south and I went north.

I got as far as the corner.

"Harry!" I yelled. "It's Joey Two Bits."

He was lying in the gutter, on his back, right outside the bar. There was a streetlight over him and it made his face yellow. His eyes were open just a slit. Harry came up behind me.

"Is he awright?" Harry said.

Harry just stood there and stared, so I bent down and touched Joey Two Bits. I laid my hand on his chest. It wasn't moving. I tried his stomach and it wasn't moving either. He didn't seem to be breathing. I leaned over him and put two fingers on his throat. No pulse. I tried not to look at his eyes, but I glanced at them and they were dull. I took my hand off his throat and just crouched there. Then I reached up and closed Joey's eyes, like a reflex, without thinking about it.

"My bes' goddamn frien'," Harry said. "I shouldna been s'mean t'him."

I stood up and put my hand on Harry's shoulder. He looked at me like I was a stranger. I went around the corner to the payphone and dialed 911. *Last round Joey Two Bits*, I thought, while I waited for a voice at the other end.

❖ ❖ ❖

The wake for Joey Two Bits was at the restaurant uptown where he worked. They had it on a Monday night, when the place was closed. They set it up in the front room at the bar and kept the other rooms dark. Finding your way back to the john was a job. I banged my shins coming and going.

I went with Harry. Everybody else where we worked was either on shift or didn't know Joey so good. Not that I knew him so good, but Harry said I had to go since I found him dead. Maybe I'm spending too much time with Harry 'cause that sort of made sense to me.

They had the coffin set up across some chairs in the middle of the room and I wasn't ready for that. I wondered if it was legal and looked around at the faces there and knew no one else cared. Lots of scars and mashed ears and bent noses. Harry and I weren't the only citizens, if you can call Harry one, but we were outnumbered.

Harry introduced me around as the guy that found Joey Two Bits dead. The first time he said that I thought no one would like me for it, but it made the guy Harry introduced me to warm right up. He was a big guy named Jimmy, he looked like that actor Chazz Palminteri. I said that later and he didn't know who I was talking about, so I told him Palminteri was a tough guy and Big Jimmy liked that.

When Harry said I was the guy who found Joey dead, Big Jimmy wanted to hear about it, so I told the story. When I got to the part about thinking "last round Joey Two Bits" while I was on 911, he laughs like to wet his pants and calls over some buddy of his and makes me tell the story again. So I tell it. And tell it. Everybody wants someone else to hear it and pretty soon everybody in the room has heard me tell the story at least once and they're all handing me drinks. I left half-finished beers and whiskeys all over the place.

It was a real crowd for Joey Two Bits, all his locales and interests represented. I met Irish boxing people and Italian waiters from Sicily and a guy from California who made wine. He talked like the Godfather. I wanted to ask him if he had toilet paper in his cheeks. I asked politer questions than that and they all treated me like a pet monkey or something, laughing at my questions and smiling at me. Big Jimmy kept smacking me on the shoulder. I played along with it and acted the young rube and it went over pretty good.

It was Big Jimmy who finally told me how Joey Two Bits got his name. He was telling some older guys a story about Joey winning some fight he was supposed to lose.

"That was back when he was Joey Quarter," Big Jimmy said.

The old guys nodded like that fixed the date, no more need be said. When Big Jimmy was done talking, I asked him what he meant about that. He grinned down at me.

"Harry never told you."

I shook my head. Big Jimmy spotted Harry at the bar and grinned at him.

"Harry probably can't remember," he said to me. "Harry, you useless bastard," he yelled across the room.

Harry nodded and lifted his glass.

"My bes' gawdam' frien'," he bawled back.

Big Jimmy shook his head at Harry and kept grinning.

"Drunk as a bishop," he said.

He turned back my direction and asked me if I know Joey Two Bits' real name. I said no. Here I am at the guy's wake, I don't even know that. Big Jimmy said it was Joseph Laughlin Quarto.

"Micks and I-tals both sides," he explains.

In boot camp, his redneck sergeant said Joey looked like an Indian and called him Chief Joseph Laughing Quarter. His platoon picked up on it, but it was too long for everyday, so it got shortened to Joey Quarter. When he was back in New York, "stinkin' up the jernt" as a boxer, his handler changed Quarter to Two Bits.

"Put some badda-bing in it," Big Jimmy said.

He made like a fighter and gave a fake jab at my chest.

"It stuck," he said. "Right up till you found him dead."

He clapped me on the shoulder again and almost knocked me down. Somebody came along and distracted him, so I went to check on Harry. I asked him how he was doing.

"My bes' gawdam' frien'," he said.

I nodded and patted him on the shoulder. He mumbled something I didn't catch. Big Jimmy and the guy he'd been talking to got everybody gathered around the coffin and they started giving toasts. After the important guys said their piece, Big Jimmy came over and asked me to say something, since I was the one who found him dead. That made sense to me too.

Big Jimmy led me around to the head of the casket and stood behind me. I lifted my beer and waited for people to shut up.

"To a stand-up guy," I said. "When he wasn't falling down."

They liked that. Big Jimmy clapped me on the shoulder for the hundredth time and sloshed some beer out of my mug and onto my shoes. I kept my glass up while the laughs faded. I put a serious face on and the place went quiet. I put my glass up higher. Everybody did the same. It felt good, I have to admit, having all these tough guys and big shots follow my lead.

"Last round Joey Two Bits," I said.

We all looked down at the coffin and said it together all at once. It was a big low murmur—"Last round Joey Two Bits." After that you could hear a pin drop. Big Jimmy cleared his throat and smacked me on the shoulder one last time. Everybody shuffled to the bar for a refill.

Harry made his way over to me. His face was all screwed up.

"Tha' was fuckin' beautiful, kid," he said.

He swayed a bit and grabbed my arm.

"Jus' fuckin' beautiful."

I took him home a little while later. We rode a cab downtown and I stood with Harry till he got the front door of his building open and made sure it was locked behind him. Then I walked uptown toward my place.

I went right past the joint where Harry and I worked, and right past the corner where Joey Two Bits died.

I didn't stop and I didn't look down in the gutter. He wasn't laying there anymore. He was in a box uptown, stretched out across some bar chairs, waiting for his wake to end. Waiting for the undertaker to plant him in the ground. Where he would wait for his boys to join him in that last round we all promised.

Chuy's Truck

It was nine o'clock when Chuy Sandoval called home. After a long hard day, he had a few drinks at Rico's, and thought better of driving. He was far too tired to walk. His wife teased him a little, then rattled down there in her old station wagon and picked him up.

"I'm glad you called me," Teresa said. "It's good you didn't drive."

"I couldn't drive if you paid me," was all Chuy said.

They drove the rest of the way without talking. It was a warm still night. Only the bugs were busy, chirping and twittering. A low dust cloud trailed out after them along the dirt roads.

Chuy had rolled a truck once, when he was much younger, after too much tequila. He drank less after that, and drove more carefully. He took very good care of this new truck. It hadn't been cheap, and the bank still owned too much of it.

Chuy woke up just after dawn. He didn't remember going to bed. He lay in the dark and thought about it for a few moments, then decided it didn't matter. While he was tying his boots, he remembered leaving his truck down at Rico's. He glanced over at Teresa. She was deep asleep.

He made coffee and checked his peppers. It was a good year for peppers. Not so good for beans. But he hadn't planted beans this year, so that was someone else's problem.

When Teresa woke up, they went back down to Rico's to get Chuy's truck. Chuy had to move some tools and supplies and he wanted to get started. An Anglo lady over in Los Ranchos hired him to patch an adobe wall that was better off torn down. Teresa wanted breakfast first, but she relented.

The truck wasn't there.

"Ah shit," was all Chuy could say. He said it several times.

"Maybe it was towed," Teresa said.

They climbed back in the old wagon and drove over to the police station. Chuy's truck hadn't been towed, so he reported it stolen. They went back home and made breakfast. Chuy picked at his food.

It was still only 7:30. He wanted to call Rico and see if the truck was there when he closed the bar, but Rico wouldn't be up till about 9:00. Chuy might as well wait till later and go talk to Rico once the bar was open. He'd be in a better way by then. Rico didn't wake up so good.

Meanwhile, Chuy could use Teresa's old wagon to shuttle things over to Los Ranchos. That Anglo lady wanted her wall fixed quick, for some big deal party. Lucky his tools weren't in the truck. He had taken them out to clean them and hadn't put them back in.

Having a plan made Chuy feel better. He told Teresa what he wanted to do while he finished his breakfast. Teresa was done eating. She was standing at the sink, washing the coffee pot.

"I need to go shopping," she said. "When can I get my car back?"

"Can't you go tomorrow? I can't get started over there till I get set up. Tomorrow morning you can just drop me off."

Teresa thought about this.

"Okay. You can have my car today."

Chuy scraped up his last bite, put his plate next to the sink, and kissed the back of Teresa's head. He went outside and began loading the wagon. He didn't want to overload the poor old thing, so he figured it would take two trips, maybe three.

It took three. It was 10:45 when he finished. He spent a few minutes examining the crumbling wall he was hired to repair, then got back in the old wagon and drove over to Rico's. Rico was behind the bar, cleaning up and restocking the liquor. He glanced toward the door when Chuy came in, but he kept working and didn't speak.

"Did you see my truck last night?"

"Wha's that?"

"Teresa came and got me last night. I left my truck here, but this morning it was gone. Did you see it last night, when you closed up?"

Rico stopped working and stood up straight. He looked at Chuy.

"You didn't come get it?"

Chuy slowly shook his head.

"Ah shit, Chuy, that's bad. It was here when I closed."

The bar was very quiet.

"You tell the cops?" Rico asked.

Chuy nodded. Rico nodded back.

"I'm sorry. That stinks. It was a real nice truck."

Chuy nodded some more. Rico offered him a beer, but Chuy declined. He shuffled out into the dirt parking lot, climbed into Teresa's station wagon, and drove back to the Anglo lady's house.

When he got there, the Anglo lady was out in the yard looking at his tools. She was one of the really strange Anglos, from New York City. She made a lot of money buying and selling stuff that other people made. Art stuff, paintings and carvings and other useless things.

"So these are the tools of your trade—eh, Chuy?"

He nodded and smiled. She had a singsong way of talking that seemed childish to him.

"Sí, señora."

Anglos like her ate that shit up. Call her "señora" and she'll never complain. She smiled broadly, her wide mouth full of big white teeth. Smiling made her eyes crinkle. She was pretty, he had to admit. But so were collies, and about as smart.

"Well, they certainly are impressive. How long have your people been making adobe?"

Long enough to know better, he wanted to say.

"A long time, señora. A very long time."

Bullshit answers like that always pleased the Anglos who were stupid enough to ask the bullshit questions. She made her toothy smile again and wandered off. *Thank God,* Chuy thought. He couldn't take her today.

He set to work, and for the first time since his truck disappeared, the moments flowed into each other without his being aware of each and every one. He didn't break for lunch till 1:30. He had meant to bring food with him, but had forgotten. He would have to go home.

But he was tired, so he took a short rest, sitting with his back against the wall, enjoying the shade from the tall cottonwoods. He squinted up into the trees. The lowest branches were twenty feet above his head and about twice that long. He loved these old cottonwoods. It irked him that the Anglo lady never seemed to notice them.

"Why do they come here?" he asked.

He climbed back in the old wagon and headed home.

❖ ❖ ❖

Chuy stopped out at the end of the Anglo lady's long dirt driveway. There was traffic on Los Ranchos Boulevard. He put Teresa's station wagon in park and waited. His thoughts were back at the crumbling wall, and what he'd have to do to keep it standing.

"She should just tear it down," he said to no one.

The speed limit on Los Ranchos Boulevard was thirty-five miles-per-hour and traffic didn't run much past that. The cops in Los Ranchos gave out tickets for anything over forty. A clump of traffic crawled by Chuy, led by a dark blue Chevy pickup.

Chuy didn't notice the truck till it was right in front of him. It was the same make and color as his, but it was a pretty popular model. He saw them all over. The driver was some punk with a blue bandana over his head. Chuy couldn't see the license plate. A green Acura was right on the truck's bumper. The punk with the blue bandana was driving slow. No ticket for him.

Chuy pulled out four cars behind. He watched the pickup truck, looked at the back of the cab over the intervening cars, studied the back of the punk's bandana-ed head. He didn't like that kid, didn't trust him driving so slow. He kept trying to see the pickup's license plate, but the green Acura hung on the truck's bumper like it was being towed.

"Can't be my truck," he said. "No one's that stupid."

The two cars in front of Chuy turned right at the next intersection. They took their time doing it and someone behind him got on their horn. Chuy glared into his rear view mirror. He was following an old white Mercedes now. It took the next left. The green Acura that was tailgating the Chevy pickup peeled off abruptly at the next right.

Chuy was following the truck driven by the kid with the blue bandana. He read the license plate. His stomach filled with acid and his hands grew sweaty.

"God damn it," he said.

His face turned to stone. His motions were slow and precise and deliberate. He put both hands on the steering wheel and turned it like an engineer carefully adjusting a valve. When they eased up to a red light about a half mile down the road, he reread the truck's license plate for the fourth time.

"God damn it," he said again.

Chuy became so still that he almost stopped breathing. Then he put the old station wagon in park, slipped out the door, and walked swiftly up the driver's side of the idling pickup. The punk with the blue bandana saw him too late and started to open his door just as Chuy got there. Chuy jerked it open, grabbed the boy's arm, pulled him out of the cab, and threw him down on the pavement. He put his boot across the boy's throat.

"Why don't you try an' guess whose truck this is," Chuy said.

The boy made a croaking sound and grabbed Chuy's boot. He pushed hard, but the older man didn't budge.

❖ ❖ ❖

The cops were there in no time. At least it seemed like no time to Chuy. It was a good thing he had reported his truck stolen, since the cops didn't much like the sight of Chuy the way they found him, standing over the punk, grinding his boot into the boy's throat. But they didn't much like the sight of the punk, either. He and the kid were both Spanish, which simplified things. Lucky the kid wasn't Anglo.

They took Chuy back to the police station and left him sitting next to a young Anglo detective's desk. The detective went off with the uniformed cop who had arrested the punk. Chuy used the detective's phone to call Teresa. She didn't answer.

Chuy felt like he was coming out of fog. He looked at the palms of his callused hands, then turned them over and put them back on his knees. He called Teresa again. He let it ring fifteen times. He was hanging up when the detective returned.

"Mr. Sandoval, do you have a ride home?"

Chuy looked up at the tall Anglo. The detective did not sit down.

"I can go?"

The detective nodded.

"Don't you want me to give a statement or something?"

The detective shook his head.

"We've got everything we need. Do you want a ride?"

Chuy made his answer very slow and clear.

"I don't need a ride. I'm going to drive my truck."

"I'm afraid we need to hold your truck."

"Why?"

The detective looked at Chuy while he picked out his words.

"He was transporting contraband and our team isn't done going over your truck yet. I'm awful sorry for the inconvenience."

Chuy took a deep breath and looked down at his hands. He raised his head and frowned at the detective.

"He stole my truck and used it to drive drugs?"

The detective shifted his weight from one foot to the other.

"Well, I didn't mention drugs, sir."

Chuy stared at him. The detective waited.

"When can I get my truck back? I need my truck."

"First thing tomorrow, Mr. Sandoval. Nine o'clock sharp. You have my word on that. Our crew will work on it tonight, everything, all the paperwork, we'll clear it up before we leave."

They watched each other.

"You can't wait here for it, Mr. Sandoval."

"I know that. I'm not stupid."

"Do you have a ride home?"

"Where is my wife's car? I was driving my wife's station wagon."

"It's back where you left it. You moved it for us. Do you remember that?"

Chuy frowned again. He vaguely remembered leaving Teresa's station wagon in a parking lot on the edge of Los Ranchos.

"Yeah. Sure. How do I get there?"

"I can drive you over."

Chuy agreed, and in a few minutes he was in an unmarked car with the detective, heading towards Los Ranchos.

"That was a very brave thing you did, Mr. Sandoval."

Chuy glanced at the cop. He was looking straight ahead, one hand on the steering wheel. He had dark glasses on.

"And also very stupid," the cop added.

"It's *my* truck."

"I understand that, sir. But that kid is a gang member. He had a pistol tucked in his belt. Did you notice that?"

Chuy hadn't seen any pistol, but he knew the cop wasn't lying. Better not tell Teresa about the pistol.

"I'm surprised he didn't shoot you," the detective said.

"Maybe he was afraid to. Maybe he thought that would make me mad."

The detective laughed, from his belly. It was a good laugh and Chuy liked him better for it. They stopped talking, and Chuy liked him for that, too.

Teresa's station wagon was in place and intact. Chuy looked at it suspiciously.

"Do you want me to follow you home?" the detective asked.

"What? Hell no. I'm all right."

"Well, if it's all the same to you, sir, I'm going to follow you home anyway. So don't run any red lights."

Chuy shrugged. It probably wasn't a bad idea.

Teresa was out in the front yard talking to a neighbor woman. She looked a little concerned to see Chuy followed by someone who was so obviously a cop. The neighbor took one look, said goodbye, and hurried off.

The detective was out of his car and next to the station wagon before Chuy even had the keys out of the ignition. Chuy stepped out and looked at his wife. She wasn't mad. That was good.

"I found my truck," he said.

Teresa raised an eyebrow.

"Ah," she said.

She put her hands on her hips and turned this way and that, making a show of looking around their dusty yard. She even stooped a little to look inside the station wagon.

"So where is it?"

The detective laughed loudly, and Chuy had to admit, the young Anglo had a real good laugh. It made Teresa smile. Chuy explained to his wife what had happened. She turned to the cop.

"Is all that true?"

"Yes, ma'am. Every word."

Teresa nodded, first at the cop, then at Chuy. She still had her hands on her hips. She turned back to the detective.

"Would you like some dinner? I'm making chicken and rice. It won't be ready for a while. If you can wait."

"Oh no, ma'am. I have to get back to work. But thank you, just the same. It's awful nice of you to ask."

Chuy liked the cop even better for not staying. Teresa smiled at them both, then turned and went inside. She always knew when to leave the men alone. They didn't talk till the screen door creaked shut.

"Thanks for following me home. I was a little shaky."

"That's all right. It was quite a day you had."

Chuy grinned and scratched the back of his head.

"Yeah, it was a day, all right. That kid can't feel too tough about now, hey? Gettin' his ass stomped by grandpa."

The cop laughed again. Chuy put his hand out and the detective took it. The young man's hand was soft and smooth.

"I'll be at your desk tomorrow morning, nine sharp. You better have my truck ready."

"It will be, Mr. Sandoval."

The detective got in his unmarked car and backed it out into the lane. Chuy was watching the car fade into its dust cloud when Teresa slipped up beside him.

"He seems nice," she said.

Chuy nodded. They stood side-by-side and watched the dust from the car rise and swirl. Then Teresa gave her husband's hand a squeeze, kissed him on the side of the chin, and went inside to make dinner.

Chuy went to check his peppers. They looked real good, firm and plump and shiny. Their stems were thick and strong and their leaves were stiff and dark. Their smell was like green apples and warm wood. He enjoyed it for a while, took deep breaths and walked slowly down the rows. Then he ambled back to the house and went inside.

He found Teresa at the kitchen sink and kissed her on the back of the head. He stood behind her for a moment, then stepped close and wrapped his arms around her. She put down her work and leaned back against him. They looked out the kitchen window at their garden.

They listened to the day fade into evening.

"It's a good year for the peppers," Chuy said.

Hungry Winter

In January, the deer disappeared. He had been eating venison since the early fall and the herds had been big and easy to find. Now they were gone.

He was working the ridge across the valley from his cabin, walking into a light wind. Low gray clouds moved over the sun. He looked up and knew they would bring more snow. He started to worry again. He hadn't seen a deer in three weeks. His stomach growled and he felt tired in his haunches.

He stopped and put his rifle down, leaned it against a tree. It went into the snow past the trigger. The snow was wearying. He looked down at his boots disappearing into it and again wished he had snowshoes.

He tried to make some a few days before. He had only succeeded in lopping off the top of the big knuckle on his left index finger. His hatchet slipped and went through his deerskin glove and through his flesh. It almost hit the bone.

The knuckle ached in the cold. The cold came in through the rough stitching he had used to patch the hole in the glove. He wrapped his other hand around the injured finger and winced. He thought about the rotten stitches he put into his ripped glove and how much better his wife would've done it.

He had been alone in these mountains almost four years. He trapped some, enough to have a little money. He didn't like it. It seemed cruel to him. He liked hunting, but he wasn't crazy for it like some men. The part he liked best was walking the ridges, but that didn't put food in your belly.

He had planned to trap more this winter. When he took his furs to town in the spring, he would use the extra money to have a good time. He was hoping to meet a woman and planning to see a whore. A woman shouldn't be as pretty as his wife, or he would lose her too, but he would like it if the whore were prettier. He had never paid for a woman before, but he had been without one four years and now he was willing.

But the heavy snows made trapping hard and he gave up on it. The snow had closed him in. As it grew deeper, his movements became smaller. He hadn't gone further than the neighboring valley since late November.

He looked out across the slope ahead. It grew steeper. The trees were younger and less frequent and rocks jutted through the snow. When the trees grew to a certain size, they fell over. The slope was littered with fallen trees, none bigger than two feet across. He decided he'd had enough and wasn't up to picking his way across this difficult place. He doubted there was any deer on the other side of it.

He lifted his rifle and turned around, going north to where he had left the trail.

A hundred yards back he found the cougar tracks. A shiver went up him, from his heels to his scalp. It was a big cat. He had seen no evidence of a mountain lion in this valley or two valleys on either side. He had seen a small lion early in September, when he was further west, trapping along a nameless stream that ran down a narrow hollow. But that cat couldn't have gotten this big in three or four months.

The tracks crossed his trail and went up the ridge. He went up after them. The cat had stopped about thirty feet on. Maybe it had watched him through the trees. A cougar could see a long way through the winter woods. He looked off toward the south, to where he had stopped maybe ten minutes earlier. The cat could have watched him from where he stood now.

He continued after the big cat. The prints ascended the ridge, then turned south. Another shiver went up him, more violent than the first. It seemed the cat was tracking him. He raised his rifle and spun around, looking wildly through the trees.

He lost his footing. He stuck his left hand out and jammed his injured knuckle into an oak. His weight went against it and the patch stitching on his deerskin glove burst. The rough bark tore open the glove and ripped his knuckle. The scab took good skin with it, then the bark went against the naked wound and took it down to the bone. Blood splattered bright red against the snow.

The shock of it silenced him. No screaming curses like those he had made when his hatchet slipped. He sat where he had fallen and wrapped his hand around the injured finger again. The dark blood came out fast and soaked into the deerskin. He saw the blood before he felt its stickiness. Soon the bleeding stopped. It was too cold for bleeding.

His head came up fast. Something brown had moved on the slope beneath him, off to his right. He caught it with the corner of his eye and his head came up before the image had registered. He knew it was the big cougar. It had circled around and was now down below him.

He let go of his finger and found his rifle in the snow. He pointed it down the slope. Nothing moved. Nothing happened. The wind picked up and the trees on the top of the ridge behind him started to howl. He got to his feet, slowly and carefully. He glanced frequently down the slope. He stood still and listened. The blood on his gloves started to freeze.

He moved slowly to the north, toward the trail he had left an hour before. He watched the slope beneath him and stopped frequently to turn and inspect the woods all around. Another violent shiver came over him. He fired a shot down the slope, hoping to scare the big cat off. Five seconds later the echo came back to him from across the valley.

The trail wasn't much easier than the raw slope. He fell once, about halfway down the ridge, and his rifle went skiing ahead of him. His bad hand broke that fall too and the bleeding started again. He scrambled down the trail after his rifle. It didn't go far. Its weight took it down into the snow. He found it jammed against a rock. He fished it out of the snow and resumed picking his way down the trail. He was more careful now.

Twenty yards down the trail and he could see the thin wisp of smoke rising from his cabin. His heart pounded and he said a small prayer. He become conscious of the fresh blood freezing around his finger and made plans for cleaning and dressing the wound.

As the trail fell, his spirits rose. He stopped to scan the woods less frequently. He did not see any more patches of brown motion off between the trees. He told himself that smart old cat took off at his warning shot.

A breeze came up and blew through the hole in his glove. He eased the aching hand into his coat pocket. He thought again about his wife and how she would have sewn the hole with careful even stitches. She could have stitched the hole in his hand the same way.

He went out into these lonely woods when his wife left. They were poor and she was pretty, and one day a rich man took notice of her. Off she went. He left town and went up into the hills. Almost four years ago. Three mild winters and now this one. Snow on the ground since October.

The snow started again when he reached the valley floor. Big flakes wobbled down in the slight wind. Soon his hat and shoulders were white. He held his rifle loosely, the barrel pointing down ahead of him. The tip of the barrel sometimes dipped into the snow.

Flat stepping stones took him across the iced-over creek. He mounted the steep bank on the other side and turned onto a side trail. He went a hundred feet and stopped inside a small clearing and looked at his log cabin. It was low-roofed, solidly built from thick logs. He was breathing hard. A cloud of steam rose from his mouth and snowflakes dusted his red cheeks. He told himself, once again, that his wife would have been proud of him for building this cabin. It was a comfortable lie.

He was stamping his feet on the flat rocks outside his cabin door when the big shiver came. He spasmed from his toes all the way to his crown. He lifted his rifle and spun around. Nothing there. The shiver was still fading, and he stood with his rifle clutched up high until it passed. He turned back to his cabin and stamped his feet one last time.

And one last time, his head came up fast. He didn't see a brown motion this time, not with any part of either eye. He didn't hear anything but the wind in the tall pines behind his cabin. If he had lived to tell it, he would not have been able to explain why he looked up when he did.

But his head jerked up and he saw the big cat dropping at him from the low roof of his cabin. His rifle didn't come up fast enough. His last shot lodged in one of the thick logs that made his cabin wall.

The cougar weighed almost twice as much as him. It snapped his neck in a few seconds. Its winter fur was thick and soft and tawny-colored. White flakes fell on its muscular back, settled in the cleft between its shoulder blades. Bright red blood splattered on the snow.

Fetch

Two men came out of a snow-covered wood. One man was short and broad shouldered, the other narrow and tall. They wore brown leather coats and dark pants. The short broad man had a blue woolen hat and carried a rifle against his shoulder. The tall narrow man wore a black pleated cap and carried two fishing rods and a knapsack.

A dog trailed behind, big and thick-chested with shaggy mud-colored fur and a long muzzle. The dog passed the men as they moved out from under the trees and into a clearing by a frozen lake. The snow was deep in the clearing so the men slowed. The dog bounded through the snow and was out on the ice before the men were halfway to it. You could see the ice where the wind had blown the snow away. The wind was gone now and it was still and quiet around the frozen lake.

The men stopped at the shoreline. The tall man laid the fishing rods in the snow and dropped his knapsack. The short man kept his rifle against his shoulder and looked across the lake. The dog turned to look at the men, then started back toward them, skidding across the ice.

The tall man opened his knapsack and brought out a stick of dynamite. He found a fuse in his bag and fitted it to the explosive. The big dog ambled up and sat panting at his feet. The tall man lit the fuse and threw the dynamite out onto the ice.

The dog ran after it. The tall man yelled at him.

"Burl, come back here! Stop, dammit!"

The dynamite landed on open ice and slid across it, spinning in lazy circles. It stopped against a patch of snow. The big dog followed, his momentum carrying him across the ice, his paws slipping only a little here and there.

"Burl, come on! Here, Burl!"

"He's not listening," the short man said.

The dog reached the dynamite and got it in his mouth. The men could see the fuse sparking and could hear its hiss in the still cold air.

"Dammit, Burl! Drop it!"

The dog started back slowly. He had no momentum to carry him, so he slipped and slid across the open ice. But each step brought more speed and greater stability.

"Aw, hell," the tall man said.

The two men stepped backwards in unison, turned simultaneously, and started to run. But the snow was deep in the clearing, piled up off the ice by the wind that had stopped, so the men moved slowly. They went only a few steps and looked over their shoulders and the big dog was already nearer. The tall man stopped running and turned back toward the ice and the dog and the hissing stick of dynamite. The short man went another two steps before he stopped too.

"How long's that fuse?" the short man asked.

"Shoot 'im," the tall man said.

They glanced at each other. The short man lifted his rifle and pulled the trigger. The shot cracked the air and boomed back from the snow-covered hills across the frozen lake. The dog's front legs folded under and he ran down into the ice. He yelped and the dynamite fell from his mouth and skidded across the ice into another patch of snow.

"Aw, Burl," the tall man said.

The dynamite never exploded. When it dropped from the dog's soft mouth and slid into the snow, the fuse went out. In the spring, when the thaw finally came, the two men buried Burl in the clearing by the lake.

Two Head Gone

It was the worst drought in a hundred years and the hottest winter anyone could remember. By noon in early January the temperature was in the eighties and at night warm winds from the south kept it above sixty. The fields were brown and yellow-gold and empty trees stood stark on the ridges against pale blue skies. Shredded clouds drifted high and slow, offering no hope of rain.

In these beautifully bleak circumstances, Harold Rhinebeck decided to sell two beef cattle. He ran forty head on borrowed land that was cropped down to dry mud and he didn't have enough cash or credit to buy more hay. He stood outside the barbed wire fence strung around the lower pasture on Rolling Cove Farm and looked at the thin grass and the thinning cows. He did the math in his head and calculated that selling two should raise enough cash to hold his finances together for another couple weeks. Hopefully by then something else would break in his favor; he had a few deals in the works. If not, he could always sell more cattle.

Harold's wife wanted him to sell the whole herd and take the loss. His pride could not accept it. Beef prices were low because of the drought. Hay went for a premium in drought years and most amateurs, people like Harold, dumped their cattle when the cost of feeding them made the hobby too expensive. Beef prices would rebound in the spring, when the grass came back and hay was no longer necessary. Harold was determined to wait. Even a small profit would justify it.

He watched the cattle pick over the shreds from the last two hay bales, big round loaves each the size of a tool shed. All that was left were scattered clumps stomped full of mud and manure. *They eat it, shit it, and eat it again*, he thought, *then we eat them.* A big cow exhaled loudly and laid down heavily in the straw and mud and manure. She closed her eyes and chewed her cud. Two other cows followed her lead. Harold shook his head, glanced at the dried fields and ridges, and got in his old Wagoneer.

He turned the car around and drove back down the dirt road that ran up the middle of Rolling Cove. He went past the entrance to Rolling Cove Farm and noted again the effects of new ownership. The house had been painted and the gutters repaired. The fruit trees on the side yard had been trimmed and a new fence started around the back pasture. He took it in and felt defeated.

Harold and his wife had owned Rolling Cove Farm for eight years. They sold it and moved at the end of the preceding summer, to a better address in a more upscale town. They were building a smaller but fancier spread that Harold was discovering they couldn't afford.

There was no room for forty head of beef cattle at his new place, or so his wife insisted, so Harold persuaded the new owners of Rolling Cove Farm to let him keep his herd there through the winter. They seemed dubious but they agreed. He did not offer to lease the land and they did not request it. At the time this windfall felt like a good omen. Now it seemed meaningless.

Harold stopped at Pete Mack's place and hired the old man to drive two head into market on Saturday. With the cash from that sale, Harold would pay Pete and buy a load of hay. Harold wanted to use his wife's horse trailer and haul the cattle himself, but he knew how she would react and it wasn't worth the grief. Harold was pleased with himself for devising this alternative plan of hiring Pete Mack, but the necessity of it shamed him. He didn't even try to fool himself into thinking that Pete didn't see through it.

Pete had an ancient pickup truck equipped for hauling cattle, fitted with high wooden sides and a wooden gate across the back. Harold stood in the old man's driveway and looked at the peach-colored and pockmarked truck. He walked around it and looked at the rusted metal and the weather-beaten wood. He felt a pinch in the pit of his stomach. He reached out and rattled the gate. He got a splinter in his index finger.

"God damn," he muttered.

He squeezed the wound and a little pearl of blood emerged. He wiped that off and found the splinter's tip. He yanked it out with his fingernails. It bled more than seemed necessary.

❖ ❖ ❖

Saturday came and Harold found Pete under the hood of his truck. The old man grinned at him.

"Jus' checkin' th' url," Pete said.

Harold nodded and said nothing. He felt that pinch in the pit of his stomach again. Pete slammed the hood and they climbed in. The engine turned over and they drove up the dirt road to Rolling Cove Farm.

Pete spent the short drive talking about the new owners and how much he liked them. He had the good grace not to mention all the improvements they had made. Harold wondered if Pete was glad the Rhinebecks had left.

They drove past the main entrance and bounced up to the gate on the lower pasture. Harold jumped out and opened the gate, Pete pulled through, Harold closed the gate and got back in the truck. They wallowed slowly across the field to where the herd stood staring at them. They stopped about thirty feet from the nearest cow, a huge black and white steer.

"Which two yuh want?" Pete asked.

Harold looked at the cows for a while. They were moving slowly toward the truck, hoping for fresh hay.

"Whichever two will get me the most money."

Pete shook his head.

"Can't take 'em in this ol' wreck."

"Why not?"

The old man squinted at the big black and white steer.

"Too heavy."

"Right. Of course."

Pete draped his arms across the steering wheel and waited. Harold felt flushed, hot on his neck and arms. He hated the whole pathetic undertaking.

"What's the best we can do?"

Pete pointed out two heifers that were standing close together. They were beautiful cows. The whole herd was prize stuff.

"Them right there. Good size, an' they'll be easy to sep'rate."

"Okay. Let's do it."

Pete cut the two cows out and Harold helped get them into the truck. Harold was determined not to get in the way and he succeeded. It didn't make him feel any better, but at least he didn't feel any worse.

The two men got back in the truck and went back out through the gate. Pete tooled down the dirt road. When he reached the end, he turned right, went about a quarter mile, then made a left onto the highway. When they were humming down the polished blacktop, the old man began to talk.

"How's the missus?"

"Fine, fine. Thanks for asking."

"Rachel and Don?"

Harold's unruly children.

"Good, good."

"Get that ridin' ring finished?"

"Yes, finally."

"Fences and stalls?"

Harold felt flushed again. His stomach started to burn.

"Well, no, actually. We have a fellow coming next week."

"I a-magine Della Anne can't wait."

Della Anne was Mrs. Rhinebeck.

"She has become a might impatient, yes."

Pete snorted, then laughed with what sounded to Harold like a trace of scorn.

"A might impatient. Yeah, I'll bet. Hee hee hee!"

Harold's ears felt hot. He wanted to defend his indefensible wife but couldn't think of anything to say. He looked out his window and saw some crows chasing a hawk. He wished the damned crows would leave the hawk alone. The birds passed from view and he was grateful, even though he could have stopped watching them whenever he wanted. He looked at the high luminous sky and felt belittled by it.

He brought his attention back to the truck and killed a few moments wishing Pete would go faster. Then he counted the rust holes on the hood and changed his mind. He imagined the old hulk breaking down along the road and had a flash of panic. But it kept humming along.

He took a deep breath and tried to get a grip on himself. It almost worked.

"I gotta get me some gas," Pete said.

"Why?"

Harold's voice came out too loud. Pete gave him a puzzled glance.

"Usual reason."

"Of course."

When they rounded the next bend, Donner's Shell Station came into view, and Pete slowed the truck. He pulled off into the station, stopped alongside the first pump, and stepped out.

Harold fumbled miserably with his door. Eventually he found the latch handle and managed to free himself. He closed the door and stood beside the truck for a moment, blinking at the glare from the chrome on the pumps. Then he shuffled about twenty feet across the cracked pavement, stood with his back to the truck, and stretched.

He put his hands up in the air and his head back. He let out a long breath and turned his head to one side and then the other. He took another deep breath. He put his hands down and looked at the sky. No clouds, just high arid blue. It occurred to him that he should pay for the gas.

The sound was so unexpected he almost didn't believe it. There was a loud sharp crack directly behind him, like a homerun hitter shattering a bat. He froze for an instant, then started to turn just as the sound came again. When it came a third time, Harold was facing the truck and saw what was happening.

One of the heifers was kicking the wooden gate that enclosed the back of the old pickup. The fourth kick split the gate wide open. The two cows stumbled out backwards, then stampeded past Harold and off into the hollow behind the station.

Harold turned to watch them go.

"Aw hell," Pete said. "God damn."

The old man took off after the cows. Harold followed behind. The station attendant watched the whole thing from the window and slowly chewed her gum, no reaction on her calm broad face.

❖ ❖ ❖

It was rough, up-and-down country. Everything was brown and gold and crackled underfoot. Their sweat disappeared into the dry air and their throats ached. Brambles and cedar needles tore at their clothes and ripped their wrists and hands. They did not talk.

The brittle vegetation left a clear record of the heifers' passing. Tall grass was knocked down and saplings were trampled. Leaves were swept away to expose the baked reddish-brown earth, gouged and dented by scrambling hooves.

They tracked the cows up the hollow, through a cove at the far end, and then they climbed into a narrow and steep little gorge that grew deeper as they ascended. It had been cut into the mountainside by a small spring, but the drought and the unseasonably warm winter had squelched the flow and left the gorge parched and empty. They found the cows about a mile from the road, where the little gorge opened up and ended.

It was a flat-bottomed, almost box-shaped space about forty feet long and wide and of slightly greater depth, with sides that were nearly vertical at the top. The only obvious evidence of the spring that began here and cut the gorge was a sheet of pale green moss dying on a large rock in the small clearing at the center of the box's floor. A partially fallen poplar on the gorge's rim formed a triangular archway high up above. Sunlight filtered in, illuminating the floating dust kicked up by the scrambling heifers.

They had tried to climb out the far end and had gotten stuck. One had her front legs folded under and wasn't moving. The other was mobile and restless, but wouldn't leave the one that was down. Pete went up to have a look. He didn't get very close before the cows started to fuss. The one that was standing almost fell. Pete came back down.

"Afraid a makin' things worse," he said.

The two men stood at the bottom of the gorge with their hands on their hips and looked up at the stuck cattle.

"Maybe we kin get above 'em an' shoo 'em down," Pete suggested.

They studied this proposal. The slope was too steep above the cows. The closest they could get would be up at the top of the gorge, which wasn't close enough.

"Ain't no way to get above 'em and be anywheres near 'em," Pete said.

Harold walked around in a little circle and looked at the ground. Pete folded his arms across his chest and watched the heifers. Harold stopped walking, looked up at the cows, checked his watch, then made another circle. At the end of it, he turned to face Pete. Fifteen seconds passed before he said anything.

"I'm gonna go call Animal Control."

Pete nodded at him.

"I'll wait for them at the gas station. Do you mind waiting here?"

Pete shook his head. Harold scrambled back down the gorge, jogged through the little cove and most the way down the hollow, then walked the last stretch to Donner's Shell Station. He stopped outside to catch his breath, then went in and asked the blank-faced girl behind the counter for change.

She pointed at the truck and made him pay for the gas and told him to move the truck out of the way. He went outside and looked for the keys. They weren't there. He went back inside and told the girl, who had no reaction, verbal or otherwise.

He took his change to the pay phone, got the number from information, and dialed.

❖ ❖ ❖

Fifteen minutes passed. Harold spent it pacing the cracked asphalt. He noticed his thirst and thought of Pete waiting out in the woods, and was just turning toward the station to buy them each a bottle of water when a beige pickup truck turned in off the highway. He forgot about his thirst when he saw the county seal on the truck's door.

The driver was a short solid woman in her mid-forties. The truck was the same color as her khaki uniform. Her shirt had the county seal on its shoulder. She pulled up next to Harold and rolled down her window.

"Mr. Rhinebeck?" she said.

He nodded. The woman parked her truck, rolled up the window, and climbed out. She reached back inside the cab and took a rifle from the gun rack.

"What's that for?" Harold asked.

The woman didn't look at him.

"In case of the worst," she replied.

She dug a box of cartridges out of a small canvas knapsack on the truck's seat. Harold watched her load the rifle. It wasn't the little twenty-two his wife kept around the farm. The woman returned the box of cartridges to the knapsack, then shrugged the bag onto her shoulders.

❖ ❖ ❖

Harold led the way up the hollow. He was tired now and the going seemed painfully slow. Every bramble caught his clothing and every step was uneven and jarring. They picked their way through the cove at the far end and climbed up into the box-shaped termination of the little gorge.

Nothing had changed, except that Pete was sitting down on a fallen tree. He rose as they approached. All three heads turned up to look at the stuck cows. Harold checked his watch. Fifty minutes had passed and the cows hadn't budged. He looked at Pete and wished he had bought those bottles of water.

The woman leaned her rifle against the log Pete had been sitting on, then dug some binoculars out of her knapsack. She left the bag next to the rifle and walked around on the floor of the gorge and looked at the heifers from various angles. She used the binoculars to study the cow that was down.

"Leg's broken," she said.

"Are you sure?" Harold asked.

The woman nodded. The three of them stood and considered the downed cow. The woman still had the binoculars in her hands. Pete had his arms folded across his chest and Harold had his hands deep in his pockets.

"I'm gonna hafta shoot 'er," the woman said.

Harold felt acid crawl up his throat.

"Why?" he croaked.

"She can't get down an' we can't get 'er down," Pete explained.

Harold stared at the woman for a moment, then sighed and shrugged.

"All right," he said quietly.

The woman returned to the fallen tree and put her binoculars back in the knapsack. She picked up the rifle and walked to a spot that offered a good clear shot of the downed cow's head. There was a small click when she turned off the rifle's safety.

She aimed the gun and pulled the trigger. The shot exploded into the box-shaped space and boomed back down the gorge and out through the cove and off into the hollow beyond. The dead cow slumped down and started to roll. It gained speed with each turn, crashing over the dead wood and dried vegetation. It stopped abruptly against a log lying just off the gorge floor.

But the crashing sounds continued. The other cow had panicked at the sound of the shot and lost its footing. They looked up just as it tilted over backwards and made a long tumble down. It was a terrible, slow motion fall. The sound of its back breaking was like a limb coming off a tree.

The worst part was that it didn't die. It lay at the bottom of the gorge and bellowed out its pain. It was almost as loud as the gun. While Harold was still trying to understand what had happened, the woman used her rifle again, and the horrible sound stopped.

Then the only sound was the second shot tearing open the air in the gorge and slamming and clamoring its way out into the hollow and away into the valley back behind them.

❖ ❖ ❖

No one said anything while the sound of the last shot was still with them. They listened to it roll and rumble out and away. When it was gone, Harold swallowed hard and made his mouth work.

"How do we get them out of here?" he asked.

The woman just looked at him. His knees went weak.

"How—how do I get the meat..."

His voice trailed off.

"They only way to get the meat is to butcher them right here."

Harold stared at the dead cows. They looked huge.

"How do we do that?"

She didn't answer right away. He watched her and waited.

"Well, Mr. Rhinebeck, you can do it yourself, or you can hire someone. But it ain't gonna pay. You'll have to haul that meat out on your back. Maybe you can get a packhorse up to the start of the gorge. It's rough country back to the road. It's a loss, sir, and I'm sorry."

She turned and left. Harold watched her go. When she was gone, he slowly turned back to look again at the dead cows. He felt he was choking and forced his dry throat to swallow.

"Damn shame," Pete said.

The old man's voice was deep and mournful. Harold nodded, and his eyes felt as if tears would come. But his eyes were as dry as his throat. He looked around at the baked woods, and felt as dry and worn out as the strange winter countryside.

In his mind, he saw the carcasses as they would be in no more than an hour, covered by the big vultures that rode the currents over the cragged ridges. They were probably on their way already. A swarm would turn in the air above for days, until only the bones and hide were left.

Then he saw his wife's new riding ring, unfinished and empty of horses, useless without fences and stalls. He knew it would stay that way till the next owner took over the property. They hadn't even been there six months yet. He looked at the dead cows and felt all his plans had died with them. He would have to call the bank soon. He felt his wife would surely leave him.

He put his hands on his knees and bent over at the waist. He wanted to be sick, but the sickness wouldn't come.

❖ ❖ ❖

Harold didn't leave the house for two days. Sometimes he would stand in the bedroom window that had the best view of the incomplete state-of-the-art riding ring and stare at it for half an hour.

He looked at the phone frequently but he didn't use it. Pete Mack called and left a message. He had replaced the gate on his truck and offered to try again, for the fee they'd discussed, no extra. Harold stood by the answering machine and listened, with his hand on the receiver, but he didn't pick it up.

Sometimes he stood in front of the liquor cabinet and looked at the bottles inside. But he didn't drink.

When forty-eight hours had passed he finally left the house late in the afternoon. He suddenly didn't want to be there when his wife got home. He put his old Wagoneer on the highway and just drove. He was almost to Yellow Well when he realized where he was going.

Donner's Shell Station was empty. He parked next to the restrooms and sat for almost a minute, staring blankly into the hollow. Then he stepped outside and started walking. The path the heifers had cut was still clear. He went up the hollow and through the cove at the far end.

He stopped outside the mouth of the narrow little gorge and remembered his first ascent into it. He remembered his legs working against the rising ground and the strange winter heat and the occasional cool of deep shade. It was merely warm today and the sun was about to set. The climb would be easier but his motivation was weaker.

He stayed where he was. He imagined the two carcasses, ripped open, dried and spared much rancidity by the arid weather, with most the soft tissue gone but still attracting carrion eaters, vultures hopping and crawling over them, with more waiting in the trees and on the ground nearby, occasionally scuffling over the choicer bits of flesh.

He looked up. In a long tall swirl over the ridge, a half dozen vultures tilted their ragged wings and marked their slow regular time. The low sun turned their lighter feathers brown-gold and their darker ones purple-black. Far behind them was the cloudless ultramarine sky.

He watched them and hated them and envied them. *We both eat cow* he thought, and half-smiled. Finally he admitted they were beautiful. He watched the highest one bank and coast and his own heart soared just a little. Then he turned and left.

He filled his tank back at the station. He paid the attendant and bought some gum. He put a quarter in the pay phone and called Pete Mack.

The Bitter Taste

He stepped through the gates and they clanged shut behind him. He didn't look back because he didn't want to remember. The bus was late so he stood in the dust and lit his last cigarette. The desert looked as mean as he used to feel. The sand and dust were baked dry and there was no wind. A raven going down the valley made the only visible movement. He swallowed some smoke and squinted at everything before him.

A wide dirt drive started at his feet and ran level for fifty yards. It dropped out of sight over the lip of a wash and reappeared on the other side, another hundred yards further on. It ran straight from the gates behind him to a two-lane state highway of fresh black asphalt that footed the hills on the far side of the valley. He watched the highway's yellow lines quiver in the heat. He took another drag. The raven was gone.

His eyes followed the highway, traced it up the valley and back down. It emerged from behind some low hills to his left, sloped its way down the valley, then slipped behind another set of even lower hills far off to his right. The low hills that fronted the highway and the tall ones behind it were all the color of sand and ash and strewn with loose charcoal gray rocks. The rocks got bigger as the valley fell.

He had gotten smaller during his time inside. When he entered prison twenty years ago, he was slight and wiry but strong for his size and vigorous. Now he stooped slightly and his knees were weak and achy. They cut cancer out of his belly ten years back and his stomach had trouble with half of what he put in it. Maybe that would change with better food, but he doubted it.

He was thirty-two when he went in and thoroughly rotten. He robbed gas stations and liquor stores and beat women. His family disowned him and his friends were worse than loneliness. Now he was fifty-two and tired. He took another drag on his Marlboro and let the smoke drift out of his nostrils. He looked out at the highway again and blinked slowly. The yellow lines still wavered.

He wrote to his family a few times, after he had been in for a couple months and was starting to crawl up the walls. He tried his mother first, then his younger brother, and finally his older sister. Nothing came back. He got along all right inside but he didn't make any friends he couldn't do without.

And now he was outside.

He dropped his butt into the dust and ground it under his heel. He held a hand up to block the sun and peered out to the highway, hoping to see the bus. The road was empty except for a brown sedan that was slowing to turn into the prison drive. He felt a pang in his chest and wished he had another smoke.

❖ ❖ ❖

She was seventeen when he sold her a dime bag of crank in a Burger King parking lot. She snorted it right there and he took her back to his place. She didn't leave till he threw her out six months later.

Thinking about it brought the sour taste to the back of his throat from that good biker speed. He stood in the dust and swallowed the remembered bitterness and stared out over the sand and dirt and rocks. He blinked at some thin gauzy clouds behind the far hills. The brown sedan completed its turn and started up the drive.

She was the best-looking girl he'd ever had, and he'd had some fine girls. He thought about her more than anyone or anything when he was inside. Hard not to think about a girl that fine when girls are what you want most. Other girls he remembered naked, all easy availability and quick access. He remembered her in a blue-gray halter top and blue jeans, running across a supermarket parking lot at sundown, her long legs going like pistons and that golden hair flying out behind her.

She was so damned beautiful it made his chest hurt. But even with looks like that he couldn't stay interested. And when he got bored he hit her. Just to spice it up. If he could get a girl like that now, he didn't think he could ever get bored. He was so soft with her at first he talked about getting married.

Christ, for another smoke, he thought. The raven came back going the other way.

She even thought it was true after he stopped talking and started hitting. He winced at the memory of it. It seemed more real than when it happened, distilled by all the times he had remembered it before. When she got pregnant, he beat her from top to bottom, dumped her back in the Burger King parking lot, and left town. He'd been meaning to go anyway.

He forgot about her for the next couple of months, while there were other girls to blot her out. When there were no other girls, she haunted him. He got drunk one night to shake her off and put himself in jail by sticking up a Gulf station. The greasemonkey behind the counter came up with a pistol, shot first and clipped him in the shoulder. He fired back fast and sloppy. He shot the cash register and the man behind it and a window behind the man. He spent two weeks in a hospital prison ward getting his shoulder patched up, then two months in the county jail. Then he was tried and convicted and sent to the state prison. The greasemonkey died on the oily floor of the first service bay. One shot through the neck.

He started thinking about her again the first day he woke up in the hospital prison ward. Sometimes he started out thinking about other girls but he usually ended up thinking about her. Sometimes he wound up thinking about the greasemonkey dead on the floor.

❖ ❖ ❖

He had been in the pen for six years when her family tracked him down. Two big Mexicans came up to him in the laundry and the bigger one mentioned her name. His heart froze in his chest. *Why Mexicans?* he wondered. *She was a white girl.*

The Mexicans gave him a message. She had people that knew what he'd done and were patient. Her people wanted the satisfaction of killing him themselves. They would wait till he was outside. Every day till then he should remember that he was a dead man. He looked up at the Mexicans' brown faces and tried to guess how they had become the messengers.

Whatta ya think I did? he said, trying to sound cool. The smaller one didn't like that and was all for killing him right there. But the bigger one was in charge and they had orders. *What'd I do*? he said to them. *What happened to her?* His voice was squeaky now. The bigger one looked almost sorry for him, shrugged enormous shoulders. The smaller Mexican glared at him, then dropped him with a punch in the face and kicked in two of his ribs. He was in the infirmary for two weeks. The ribs were slow to heal.

He asked around and learned the Mexicans' names. The smaller one was called Crio. Crio caught another conviction and become a lifer, then got stabbed and was moved to another prison, got stabbed again and died. The bigger one was Max. Ten years ago, when he got his belly cancer cut out, Max was in the next bed with kidney stones. Demerol made the big Mexican talkative. He learned that the girl's brother worked with the Mexicans dealing smack. He tried to learn more but that was all Max said before the dope knocked him out.

Max was paroled eight years ago. The last time he saw Max, the big Mexican grabbed his shoulder and told him not to forget that message from the girl's family. The big brown man seemed like a priest somehow and he suddenly felt desperate for Max's approval. *How can I forget?* he said. *I can't never forget.*

And now he was outside.

❖ ❖ ❖

He watched the brown sedan come up the drive and wondered what was taking so long. It seemed to be moving fast enough but it didn't seem to be getting any closer. He eyes caught yellow motion out on the highway. It was the bus, slowing down as it approached the prison drive. He watched it longingly for a moment, then brought his eyes back to the brown sedan. The sedan finally disappeared onto the slope that climbed toward the prison.

He looked out to the highway again, saw the bus was swinging hard into the dirt drive. He wondered who the driver was. Couldn't be anyone he knew, but he wondered anyway. He rubbed his mouth with the edge of his hand and took a long breath, then put his eyes on the lip of the slope and waited.

He saw a heat shimmer first, then the brown roof became visible, then the body of the sedan popped up over the lip of the wash, fifty yards away and closing fast, trailing dust and spitting pebbles. It swung around to his left, off the packed dirt and gravel of the prison drive and onto the sandy desert floor. The sound the tires made changed abruptly, from a hammering rumble to a sharp hiss. It circled toward him and pulled to a stop at his feet. The passenger side was facing him.

Dust blew off the car and into his face. He blinked and wiped his mouth with the back of his hand. The passenger window whirred down and a blond man showed him a pistol. The man held the gun in his left hand, along his left thigh. He looked at the pistol, then brought his eyes up to the man's face. It was wide with prominent cheekbones, a male version of the girl's face. He looked into hazel eyes that were cold and hard, not the deep shining ones he missed. Then he looked down and smiled at the gun. *Where have you been?* he thought. *Who have you killed?*

The man mentioned the girl's name. He stopped smiling and nodded once. The man brought the pistol up and pointed it at his chest. He sighed and wanted one more smoke very badly. The man looked at him like he was supposed to run. He couldn't run if he wanted to. His knees hurt too much and his stomach was a bag of acid.

"Christ, get on with it," he said.

The blond man pulled the trigger. He heard the retort and felt the first bullet crack his sternum. The ones that followed didn't matter. Everything went numb below his shoulders. He lay on the ground on his back and the dust cloud from the departing brown sedan settled on his clothes.

He looked up at the hot sky. There were no clouds, just a blue-white glare that hurt his eyes. He looked at it anyway. A raven appeared, high overhead, going slowly down the valley. Its wings moved in big deliberate strokes, like oars on a rowboat. He watched its progress with short labored movements of his eyes. When the raven was gone he let his eyelids slide shut. He couldn't tell if he was breathing. He wondered if he would be gone before the bus came. He didn't hear it grinding to a halt, didn't hear the driver's footsteps crunching toward him.

He saw her again. He saw her running and wanted to follow. Blue-gray halter top and blue jeans, long legs like pistons, golden hair streaming like a flag.

The bitter taste came into his throat.

The Waving Man

Clay Yates stood on the wooden deck that overlooked his sloping backyard and watched the smoke from his cigar spiral through the moonlight that slanted over his roof. He lifted his martini, took a slow precise sip, then carefully returned the glass to its assigned spot on the flat wooden railing. He ran his tongue around inside his mouth, searching the heaviness of tobacco and gin. His eyes were growing bloodshot.

Yates served Virginia's 5th District in the United States Congress. He was a popular New Republican, elected by a wide margin, with polls so high he was considered undefeatable. He was an outspoken advocate of the death penalty, on several occasions having publicly stated that capital punishment was under-utilized and should be strictly enforced. In his standard stump speech, Yates quoted "an eye for an eye, a tooth for a tooth" when he advocated society's right to end the lives of its members. He had done so that morning, in front of a television camera, while standing under a blue banner bordered with red stars and bearing in white lettering his campaign slogan: "Faith, Freedom, and Folks."

Clay Yates was also a black man. And as of 4:30 that September afternoon, his mother was dead, and his father was a murderer.

❖ ❖ ❖

Clay's sister Pearl heard the gunshot. It came from her parents' house next door and rattled the window over her kitchen sink. Pearl froze for a second, then ran out the back door and across the rolling yards. She found her mother slumped in a metal chair on their parents' back porch. Pearl started running again and found her father around the far side of the house. He was sitting in his truck, drunk, with his shotgun leaning against the passenger seat, its barrel slanted down to the floor. Pearl ran back to her house and dialed 911, told the dispatcher where she was and what she knew. Then she called Clay and started to wail.

Clay tried to calm his sister, with little success. He coaxed her off the line and called the top criminal lawyer in Ralliston, a well-connected white man, and drove to the county jail. The lawyer beat him there. The police brought his father in fifteen minutes later. Clay waited for another ten minutes while the lawyer talked with his father, then waited another half hour while his father gave his statement to the police. Finally the police put Clay and his father and the lawyer together in a room and left them alone.

Clay's father looked shrunken and blurred and suddenly too old for his sixty-seven years.

"Why did you shoot her?" Clay said.

His father put his head down and didn't answer. Clay wiped his eyes with the back of his hand.

"I'm trying real hard not to hate you," Clay said.

He wiped his eyes again.

"Lord give me strength."

His father raised his head then, and looked at Clay with dead eyes, eyes buried way back in the cave of his soul. Clay tried to fill his heart with righteousness, but in his chest there was a fist of ice, and his hollow stomach burned.

❖ ❖ ❖

Clay drew on his cigar and held the smoke in his mouth. His martini was gone and he wanted another, but the house was full of grieving women and he was afraid to go inside. His four sisters were there, and two female cousins, and his spinster aunt. Clay blew the smoke out in little puffs and thought about his sisters. He was the youngest, had no brothers, and had no brothers-in-law.

Pearl had never married. She lived with their spinster aunt, in the old woman's rundown clapboard house next door to their parents. His other three sisters had all married, and all had done it badly. One worthless husband died in a drunken car wreck, one stole from his employer and went to jail, and the third ran off with a married woman he met at AA. When Clay argued vociferously for legislation to punish deadbeat dads, it was the fathers of his nieces and nephews he was yelling about. Clay was embarrassed by his sisters' ex-husbands, by their lack of current husbands, and by their fatherless children.

His sisters had brought most their children with them. Clay couldn't keep track of them all. His wife would add the nieces and nephews to their own children and manage the whole crowd, sisters and cousins and assorted kids and the old spinster aunt. She would feed them, medicate them, put up bedding for those who stayed the night. He would stand outside and occasionally look in, see them moving around in the lighted windows.

Pearl was in bad shape. The police found her passed out at the bottom of their parents' back steps, her forehead split open. When she hung up with Clay, she went back next door, got as far as the steps and fainted. Now she had stitches and they were gruesome. Clay couldn't look at her. He told himself it was just the way the stitches marred her pretty face, but it was really the way her eyes so nakedly displayed her panic.

He looked at his cigar and decided it was still long enough to justify that second martini. He left the cigar on the deck railing, went quietly in the kitchen door, and carefully assembled his drink, with a minimum of noise and movement. He listened to the women's voices drifting in from the living room, heard Pearl start to cry again. He dropped two olives into thick cold liquor, capped the jar and returned it to the refrigerator, picked up the iced glass, and savored the reassuring chill it applied to his fingertips. He slipped back outside, set the martini down on the deck railing, and re-lit his cigar. Once again he watched the smoke curl and twist in the cool scrutiny of autumn moonlight.

❖ ❖ ❖

Clay's father's name was Vernon and his mother's name was Celia. Vernon Yates was a big humorless man who got ugly drunk a few times a year and would sometimes smack Celia around. Celia was a shy woman, easily tongue-tied around strangers and sometimes around her own family.

Vernon broke Celia's hand four years ago. She told everyone she fell, but it happened while Vernon was on a drunk, so everyone knew what really happened. When his next drunk came around, Vernon threatened to break Celia's other hand while Pearl was trying to get her mother out of the house. They all knew what Vernon could be like when he drank. But no one did anything. Clay knew, and he didn't do anything, because he didn't know what to do. No one knew what to do. When the police left Clay alone with his father and the white lawyer, Clay sat on that hard metal chair in that desolate room at the county jail and hated himself almost as much as he hated the broken old thing across the table.

Eventually Vernon did say what happened, and the old man remembered it too well, despite the drink and the shock and the shame. He had some friends over and they were playing cards and drinking whiskey. His drinking buddies hadn't come over in years and he wanted it to be like the old times, when Celia would wait on them while they played, cook for them and serve them and never say boo.

He wanted it to be like it was before Celia lost her sight. When she first complained about her eyes, Vernon told her she was imagining things, that there was nothing wrong with them, right up till they started to fail. Then he took her into Ralliston and the doctor said it was too late. Vernon drove Celia home, helped her into the house, said he needed something at the store, and disappeared for two weeks. He lost his job and had to take a reduced pension. He missed the full pension by less than two years. He disappeared for another week when he found out.

Clay tried to get Celia to the doctor when she started complaining about her eyes. But she wouldn't go as long as Vernon said not to.

Oh no I won't, she said. *It'll make your daddy mad.*

Clay spat off the deck.

"God, Momma, how I wish you'd gone," he said.

The cigar was growing short and the smoke was pungent and getting hot. Clay found cigars especially satisfying toward the end; he wished a cigar could go on just like this forever. He drained the final sip from the second martini, but saved the olives for a last clean taste after he was done smoking.

Celia kept cooking after her eyes went. At first she burned herself and scars sprouted on her hands and forearms. After a little while she got the hang of it and she kept herself and Vernon fed. But it wasn't like before, when she cooked all the time just for the pleasure of it. It was work now, hard work for a blind old woman.

So Vernon's drinking friends were over, and they were getting drunk and cheating at cards, and Celia tried to make them dinner. But she wasn't feeling well, and she dropped a pot of turnip greens on the kitchen floor and slipped in the mess and fell.

You better do somethin' with her, Vernon, one of his buddies said.

Vernon ignored their laughter and got Celia out the kitchen door and into a chair on the back porch.

She wasn't walking right, but she didn't complain. Then he mopped up the greens and went back to the card table. They played out the hand, Vernon lost a few dollars, and Celia started calling him from the porch. He tried to ignore her.

Vernon? Could you help me, please?

The dealer held the cards and they all looked at Vernon. Celia called again.

Vernon? Could you help me, please? I'm hurtin'.

He looked at his buddies.

You better do somethin' with her, Vernon, the same buddy said again.

Vernon turned and looked at this man.

You're right, he said. *And I damned well will.*

That's when he got his shotgun and went out on the back porch.

❖ ❖ ❖

Clay found his cigar had gone out. It was too short to light again, so he tossed the stub into the bushes. He raised the martini glass and spilled the olives into his mouth, chewed them slowly and thoroughly, letting the pickling and the trace of alcohol clean some of the smoke from his palate. He swallowed, coughed a bit against the back of his hand, and looked up at the heavens. He found the big dipper splayed across the sky and tried to remember who had first shown it to him. Probably his father. Vernon knew the night sky well, better then anyone else Clay ever met.

When he went inside, the house was quiet. He was halfway across the kitchen when the phone rang. He had been avoiding it all night, told his wife he wouldn't talk to anyone but family and the law. No reporters, no politicians, no political handlers. He stopped and waited for it to ring again, and when it did, he moved over to the white wall-mounted unit and slowly lifted the receiver.

"Hello."

"Clay, is that you?"

It was a male voice, high and nasal.

"Hello, Justin."

"I've been trying to reach you all night."

"I'm sure you have."

There was a long pause. Clay breathed heavily into the receiver, tasted the tobacco and gin on his lips and tongue. He looked at his empty martini glass and wondered if a third would be a bad idea. Justin Wall was his campaign manager, a cherubic-looking white boy with a Yale degree and autographed photos of Ronald Reagan and George W. Bush hanging on his office wall.

Clay hadn't paid much attention to the photographs before his sister Pearl came by the campaign headquarters. It was late and the place was empty. Pearl wandered around while Clay got ready to go. He found her in Justin's office, standing in front of the photographs, her head tilted slightly, her hands crossed in front of her, her purse dangling from her crossed hands.

"Isn't that nice," she said. "He has a picture of the president who made movies with monkeys, and he has a picture of the president who looks like a monkey."

Clay laughed despite himself.

"You're bad, Sister," he said.

"No," she said. "Just a Democrat."

Now Clay couldn't enter Justin's office without eying those photos and thinking of Pearl.

"We need to talk," Justin said. "The press is all over me."

Clay glanced at the clock and the time didn't register, so he looked at it again. It was a little before 10:00. He moved his eyes back down to the martini glass and decided another would definitely be too many. His bones felt heavy and his muscles were stiff. He moved to the sink and put the empty glass on the counter.

"I can't talk now," he said.

"They've got hard questions, Clay. This situation impacts our core issues—"

"You think I don't know that?"

Clay shifted the receiver to his left hand, turned on the cold water and splashed a little on his forehead. Justin was silent.

"I can't talk strategy now. I can't even think about it."

Justin didn't reply. The silence grew up between them. Clay stared out the window above the kitchen sink, into the pool of light that fell on the deck. He heard a high faint wailing somewhere outside and wondered if it was a shriek owl or his imagination. He looked down and tapped his index finger on the countertop.

"It's terrible, Justin. I feel awful."

"I'm so sorry, Clay. I can't imagine what you're all goin' through. I'm really sorry."

Clay listened to Justin's breathing. It was a soft papery sound. Justin cleared his throat.

"Believe me, Clay, I don't want to do this. But the reporters—"

"The decent thing for the reporters to do, the *Christian* thing for them to do, is to leave me and my family alone in our time of grief."

Clay heard the wailing again. He looked up and peered outside.

"Tell them to leave us in peace," he said.

Justin sighed, a long hiss that crackled in Clay's ear.

"Of course, Clay. But they won't. You know that."

❖ ❖ ❖

He found his wife in bed, watching the news. He sat on the edge of the mattress and took off his shoes, then turned and leaned back against the headboard. His wife took his hand. The news anchor, a thickset white man with black hair, said something. A commercial started and finished, another came and went, then the anchor reappeared and said a few more words.

When the anchor was done talking, the screen cut to a woman reporter standing outside a small prefabricated building that looked familiar. When Clay saw who was standing next to the reporter, he realized the TV crew was outside the Yellow Well Post Office. The reporter was going to interview the Yellow Well postmistress, a pretty pixie-faced black woman who didn't look her fifty-some years. Clay didn't catch the reporter's question, but the postmistress answered in a clear strong voice.

"She was a real nice woman, real friendly. Cooked all the time 'fore she lost her sight. Neighborhood kids was always over there, eatin' goodies, even after her kids was all grown. That woman had biscuits comin' outta the oven twice a day, best biscuits you ever had too."

"They were damn fine biscuits," Clay heard himself say.

"What's that, dear?" his wife asked.

He shook his head. His wife squeezed his hand. The reporter was asking the postmistress about Vernon. She looked thoughtful while she framed her answer.

"He's a good man most the time. Always been someone you could count on to help out."

She pointed off camera.

"Cooks hamburgs down at the ball park."

The reporter asked if Vernon was ever violent. The postmistress frowned.

"When he drinks, he gets mean sometimes. I heard he hit her sometimes."

She paused.

"People was afraid of him when he drank."

❖ ❖ ❖

In the morning, Clay didn't remember getting ready for bed. He lifted an arm from under the covers and verified that he was wearing pajamas. He ran his tongue over his teeth and they felt like he had brushed them.

He looked at the clock and it said 5:03. He put his feet on the floor and found his slippers. He pulled on his robe as he went down the stairs. He found Pearl in the kitchen, leaning over the coffee maker.

"Good morning, Pearl. Did you sleep all right?"

She looked at him and Clay turned away. Her stitches were too much this early.

"What do *you* think?" she said.

Clay nodded and put his hands in his robe pockets. Pearl turned back to the coffee machine.

She was the youngest of his sisters, the one closest in age and furthest in spirit. She was the prettiest woman in Innesbelle County and could have had her pick of men, some of them rich and more than a few of them white. Clay knew she saw men, more men than he wanted to know about. The scar growing on her forehead seemed an insult from God, given all he had to bear. He looked at her, but he had to grimace to do it.

"I'm sorry you had to find her," he said.

Pearl shrugged.

"Might as well be me as anyone. Bet you're glad it wasn't *you*."

He didn't know what to say. He couldn't look at her anymore.

"Hmm," Pearl said. "I thought so."

She finished with the coffee maker. It started to hiss and spurt. Clay stared at it.

She's right, he thought. *I am glad it wasn't me.*

❖ ❖ ❖

He meant to stay home, to be with his family, but he left the house even earlier than usual. A television van came up their dirt road as he was going down it. He saw the van's brake lights in his rear view mirror. It caught up with him out on the highway, but he wasn't going to risk a speeding ticket. That was all he needed right now. He was sure to get some hard-ass state trooper. They were very tough about moving violations on Route 29 north of Yellow Well.

Last night, standing on his back deck, cigar and martini in hand, he had briefly considered what the reporters might ask. Now he looked at the dark shape looming in his mirror, the cluster of antennas on its roof silhouetted against the pre-dawn sky, and considered it again. But his mind wouldn't stay focused. He went past Route 64 and took Fontenbleau Avenue. He rolled slowly through the student housing, past the campus and the hospital, down

Main Street, over the big railroad bridge in front of the Amtrak station. He went down past the Omega Hotel and climbed up Turpentine Hill. While he drove, he tried to think, but the thinking didn't go very well.

He anticipated the scope of his error when he saw another TV van parked at the corner of 3rd Street. He turned onto 3rd and vans lined the block. Figures were clumped together and hunched over coffee cups in the morning darkness, cameras and lights and equipment bags clustered at their feet. His stomach ached. He was going against the enemy unprepared. He was a fool not to talk it over with Justin Wall when he had a chance.

He always got to work when this side street was empty and now he didn't know where to park. He drove slowly. The first reporter to spot him was a little rabbity-looking white woman who pointed at his car and yelled at her camera crew. It was the same woman who had interviewed Yellow Well's postmistress. He pulled to the curb at the end of the block, tucked his big car into the last parking space. The little reporter woman was out in front of the crowd, scurrying his direction. He saw her coming in his side mirror and thought she looked like a rat in an alley. Men with equipment jogged past her and took up positions around his car. They turned on their lamps, creating a pool of harsh white light. When he stepped out into it, Clay almost hit his chin on the rodent woman's microphone.

"Representative Yates, should your father face the death penalty?"

He stared in her direction and swallowed. He couldn't see her clearly in the glare, couldn't see anything past the lights. Her question, an obvious one, perhaps the most obvious one, was not one Clay had considered in his scanty preparations. This was the moment his campaign manager had tried to save him from, the moment he told himself he wanted to avoid. But he had put himself out in the open where they were waiting to tear him apart. *What am I doing here?* he asked himself. *Why don't I just leave?*

Then the reporter's question returned, not as a political point to be handled, but as an urgent moral dilemma. This dilemma had flitted through his mind early the night before, but he had brushed it off. Too much to deal with. Pour a martini, light a cigar. He smiled nervously at the reporter, realized that was not appropriate, and made his face grave. If unassailable as a moral issue, it must be tackled as a political point. *That's for a jury to decide*, said a little voice in his head, a high nasal voice like Justin Wall's. He opened his mouth but couldn't repeat it. *No comment*, the little voice tried again. That was even worse.

"I, ah, I feel—"

He felt cold and hollow inside.

"My father is—"

He moved his head around, tried to see faces through the searing light. He coughed into his hand and his chest felt heavy. He tasted last night's cigar and it surprised him. He coughed some more and the taste passed.

"Representative Yates?"

It was the rabbity little reporter. He looked her direction, still couldn't see her. He still couldn't see anyone. The lights burned his eyes.

"He's a good man," Clay said, his voice low and somber.

Momma was gone. Daddy was in jail. Pearl had ugly stitches across her high fair forehead.

"My father is a good man. That's all I can say about him."

His voice remained low and quiet. He heard feet shuffling. Someone muffled a cough.

"My mother is gone. We've lost her. Lost one parent already."

The reporters and the camera crews stopped fidgeting. They listened and watched and the morning silence was all around them. The sky was paling in the east. The stillness broke momentarily when birds chirped and stirred in a big tree on the other side of the street. Clay lifted his face toward their sounds. He blinked several times and each time the lights seemed brighter. His eyes became unfocused. All he could see was a white glare. His face was wide and empty and exhausted.

"My momma taught me about God," he heard himself say. "I miss her *so* much."

❖ ❖ ❖

Clay got back in his car. The reporters didn't ask any more questions. Clay drove through Ralliston the same way he came. He assumed the news people would follow, but no TV vans appeared in his mirrors. He took a long breath and wondered how he would handle himself the next time a microphone was shoved in his face.

He rolled slowly through town and onto 29 South and still there were no vans behind him. There was little traffic going his direction, but the morning rush filled the northbound lanes. He watched the road and the approaching cars and his mind wandered. Little pieces of what had happened flashed in his mind. He remembered how his father looked at the police station. He remembered last night's call from his campaign manager and wanted to punch the white boy in his button nose.

Clay was halfway home when he noticed his campaign signs were bent over. The signs were scattered up and down Route 29, stuck in the dirt along the sides of the road and in the strip of land that separated the north and southbound lanes. He thought they had been vandalized till he noticed all the other candidates' signs were bent over too. There must have been wind last night, after he went to bed. He made a mental note to call his campaign manager and tell the white boy to have someone straighten them up.

He came over the crest of a hill. Down at the bottom, in a wide grassy section of the median, there was a long row of his campaign signs, followed by a matching row of his Democratic opponent's. All but the nearest few of his signs were nearly flattened. His opponent's signs were mostly standing. As he approached the signs, Clay took his foot off the gas and hesitated, then he checked his mirrors and pulled across the left lane, off the blacktop, and onto the grass. He sat in his car and looked at the nearest sign. His name and slogan appeared in white letters against a blue background with a border of red stars. The design still moved him.

As he stepped from his car, a horn honked. He looked over to see a white man in a northbound SUV waving at him. Clay gave his political smile and waved back and wondered if he knew the man. Probably a supporter he had met at one event or another. The

SUV had one of his campaign stickers on its bumper, the same basic design as the signs he wanted to straighten up.

He turned back toward the signs and another horn honked. An older black woman in a blue sedan had her hand up and was smiling at him. He put his hand back up and smiled too. The drivers of the next two cars waved also, so he kept his hand in the air. People kept waving. Every now and then someone would honk. Clay forgot about his signs and he forgot about the reporters. He even forgot about his campaign manager.

A small station wagon passed with a little blond girl in the back seat. Clay grinned for her and waved extra hard. She grinned back and waved furiously, her hand a little blur. The next car was a big new cream-colored Cadillac with four white adults in it. Clay was still grinning for the little blond girl. An overweight middle-aged woman in the front passenger's seat of the Cadillac thought he was grinning at her. She waved back tentatively and turned to watch Clay as they passed. He was waving at someone else now.

"Who on earth is that?" the woman asked.

The answer came from a pale old shriveled man slumped down in the back seat of the big car.

"Jus' some cra-a-a-zy niggah."

The woman in the front seat looked at him over her shoulder.

"Daddy, I wish you wouldn't talk like that."

"Well I wish he wouldn't wave like that."

Everyone in the car laughed. Clay Yates smiled and waved. The Cadillac went up the hill and around the bend and out of sight.

An hour later, Clay was still smiling and waving when the first TV van came around the bend and started down the long hill. He didn't notice the van till it pulled onto the median behind his car. He glanced at it over his shoulder, then turned back to the traffic headed north. He never stopped waving.

Representative Yates was the lead item on the evening news all over the country. Most news organizations showed Clay struggling with the rabbity woman's question. Some used soundless images of his drained face behind a cluster of microphones. They all showed Clay standing next to his row of bent-over campaign signs, grinning hysterically, his eyes shining and his white teeth gleaming. They all showed the Representative waving like a crazy man.

❖ ❖ ❖

When the elections were over, and he no longer represented Virginia's 5th Congressional District, Clay Yates retreated. The local Republican leaders asked him to "assume a low profile" and he knew that meant no profile at all. He had a law degree he had never used—he went from the military into law school and from law school into politics—so now Clay joined a legal firm in Ralliston. His new partners had hoped he would exploit his political connections, but he did not, and he turned down more cases than was considered reasonable.

He spent more time with his family, but said less. He spoke less in all situations. He helped with his son's baseball team, but would not accept a coaching position. He spent more time at church activities, but declined any leadership role. He sang in the choir, as his mother used to do. Or at least he appeared to—no one could distinguish his voice from the others, and his voice had once carried.

All of this troubled his family and friends. But what troubled them most was a habit he developed about six months after the election. Clay would dress in a good suit, walk down the long dirt drive that led from his house to Route 29, cross the southbound lanes to the median strip, and stand in the grass, smiling and waving at passing vehicles. Drivers honked and waved, Clay waved and grinned back, and time melted away. He timed his sessions for the afternoon rush hour and tried to be out there at least once a week, usually twice, sometimes every weekday. Soon commuters were stopping to chat. He became a fixture in Yellow Well, the waving man.

When asked why he did it, Clay said it made people feel good. None of his family and friends could bring themselves to tell Clay how it made them feel.

No Mix

Rico was alone in his bar. Monday night's customers came early and left early, and Rico knew he should close and go home. But his mind was elsewhere so he puttered around and got no closer to leaving. The three front windows stood open and the quiet inside seemed to draw the night sounds in. The bugs sounded like they were under the tables and chairs and a passing car seemed to go right through the room.

Rico was thinking about a woman he didn't expect to see again. What could a rich Anglo lady want with a Spanish barkeep that one night together didn't satisfy? He had called her anyway and left a message she didn't return. And now he kept his bar open too late, in case she wanted a drink.

The phone rang. Rico glanced down the bar toward it and let it ring again. The phone was under the bar top next to the cash register. It rang once more before he draped his wipe rag over his shoulder, lifted the telephone onto the bar top and the receiver to his ear.

"Rico," was all he said.

It was all he ever said when he answered the phone.

"Hello, Rico," a woman's voice replied.

Rico smiled across the empty room. His smile went all the way out the open front windows.

"Madilyn."

"You remember! I'm flattered."

"Of course I remember, señorita. You are unforgettable. But I had given up on hearing from you."

"I thought the gentleman was supposed to call the lady."

Rico's big smile faded and his brows bunched together. He put his free hand on the edge of the bar and leaned against it.

"I did!"

"You did not."

"I left a message on your machine."

He heard only her breath at the other end. Rico dropped his head and frowned at his shoes. When she spoke, her words came too quickly—he heard "that was Sue" and knew it couldn't be right. He hoped she would say more, but he heard only her breath again. It stirred him. He felt a warm flush.

"I'm sorry?" Rico said. "What did you say?"

"The message was all garbled."

She paused and sighed and sighed again. Rico knew it was all for effect, but these little efforts were wanted and appreciated.

"I didn't understand that was you," Madilyn cooed.

Rico lifted his head and sent his big smile back out across the room. He laughed into the telephone.

"Maybe you need a new answering machine."

"Maybe I do."

He looked out his front windows and thought how nice it would be to see the grill of her Audi pulling up next to the door.

"Meanwhile, you should come down here and let me make you a margarita."

"Maybe I should."

"You definitely should."

His smile faded again when she did not respond. He pushed off from the bar and stood upright. He squared his shoulders.

"Madilyn?"

"Rico, I'd love to see you tonight. But I just can't. I have so much to do in the morning. That's why I called. Are you busy Friday night?"

Just the corners of his mouth turned up and his eyes sparkled only a little.

"As busy as my customers make me."

"Right. I should have thought of that. Friday's a big bar night."

"Why do you ask?"

She was slow with her answer, and if silence over a telephone line can be flirtatious, she made it so.

"I'm having a party," she said. "And I want you to come."

❖ ❖ ❖

Tuesday was gray and moody. Rico was half gone. It was good to be wanted again by such a woman and the day seemed tedious in comparison. He felt sweet and warm but his nerves were short, like he drank too much coffee but it hadn't woken him up.

"A party?" Chuy said. "At her house?"

Rico stood behind his bar and nodded across it at his friend. Chuy stared back at him.

"I guess that's the big party she's been planning," Chuy said.

Rico nodded again.

"You going?"

Rico shrugged his shoulders. He was a tall man and the shoulders were broad. It took them awhile to go up and down.

"I want to see her again. How can I see her again if I won't go to her party?"

Rico watched Chuy fidget with his beer. Someone coughed in the far corner toward the restrooms. Rico looked up at the sound and watched a middle-aged Spanish man take his hand away from his mouth.

"You could make an excuse," Chuy said.

Rico looked at him.

"I already said yes."

Chuy fidgeted some more. He smiled slyly up at Rico.

"You like her, huh?"

Rico hesitated. He squinted out the front windows at the glare that filled the parking lot.

"Sure," he said.

"That's it? Just 'sure'?"

Rico moved a few steps away from Chuy and pretended to lose interest. He glanced around the room. A few regulars dragging out their lunch hour. Nothing that needed his attention.

"Yeah—I like her. That's not enough?"

"She's a crazy rich Anglo. You gonna get involved with her?"

Rico shot Chuy a hard cold look. Chuy laughed at him.

"I guess you already are," Chuy said.

❖ ❖ ❖

It was a perfect night for a party. At five o'clock a thunderstorm came in from the southwest and spent an hour wiping the skies and streets. It was not big enough or wet enough to herald the monsoons, but it dampened down the dust and left behind clean air that was almost cool and a cluster of clouds on the western horizon that turned the sunset orange and red.

There was just a thin rose stripe left across the bottom of the sky when Rico turned into Madilyn's drive. He parked about halfway to her house, at the end of a line of cars that stretched away from the front wall. The moon was past half-full and high overhead. Rico looked up at it and felt alone and walked along the line of cars and through the open wooden gate and into the enclosed yard. He found six more cars jammed onto the gravel drive inside the walls.

The sounds of the party came to him over the roof of the house. He stopped to listen. There was soft tinkling piano jazz and the scratch and buzz of conversation. Above it came a laugh he knew was Madilyn's, a near-bray with odd musical tones. He guessed correctly that the party was centered on her deep back porch.

Rico looked up again at the high remote moon. He took a few steps sideways to see it clearly through a gap in the branches of an old cottonwood. He was not ready to enter the crowd, to meet and be introduced and feel trapped in conversation.

He walked along the front wall and looked for the spot that Chuy had rebuilt. Madilyn wanted it fixed in time for tonight's big party and had paid well for it. Late one morning, she had offered herself to Chuy, had lured him into a bedroom and stood naked before him. Rico had managed not to think about that until this moment. He felt a jolt in his guts when he let the thought in.

The patch Chuy made was barely visible in the near dark. Rico ran his hand over the wall and could feel the fresh adobe, rough and cool compared to the old worn surface. He stood with his hand against it and considered how his friend who had worked here must feel about this presumptuous Anglo woman Rico had slept with. He knew it did not matter, that Chuy understood where a man's need could lead him. Rico was not over-proud, and he was too old to be ashamed.

He turned from the wall, glanced at the lordly moon through the shroud of the ancient cottonwoods, and crossed the short distance to the party.

❖ ❖ ❖

The porch ran the length of the main section of the old adobe house. It was enclosed at each end by the house's two wing sections and opened on a courtyard planted with flowers. It had a roof about ten feet high, supported by heavy timbers, and a floor of the same glazed bricks the color of dried blood that were used throughout the old adobe house.

There was a portable bar set up at one end of the porch with a stiff-backed young Anglo man standing behind it. A buffet table stood next to him. The young Anglo wore a flowing white shirt and black pants. Waiters and waitresses dressed in the same outfit circulated with trays of food and drink. The porch was full to overflowing and Rico had passed more guests inside.

He found Madilyn where he expected her to be, in the center of the porch, in the middle of the action. Her pale skin glowed against a short black dress that clung to her curves and made her look even taller. Her straight brown hair hung loose against her shoulders and her blue eyes flashed in her long face. She laughed loudly and her even white teeth glistened when she threw her head back.

Rico watched her laugh and remembered her laughing in bed after they were together. He wanted to have that moment again. He remembered how her wide mouth felt when he kissed it.

Madilyn saw him a moment after he saw her. She smiled and waved him over. He made his way past people drinking and eating and talking and smoking. People smiled at him and people ignored him. He bumped into people and was bumped into.

Madilyn was talking to a small thin man in a charcoal gray suit and a turquoise-colored tie. The suit appeared hot and uncomfortable to Rico but the man wearing it looked cool and amused. He had white hair and surprised white eyebrows and large glistening black eyes behind translucent plastic eyeglasses with oval lenses. His face was wide and his chin was pointed. His nose was sharp and his mouth was thin-lipped and narrow. His right hand held a tumbler of opaque fluid and ice.

"Hello Rico!" Madilyn called out.

She took his hand and pecked him on the cheek and turned back to the small man in the suit.

"Wallace, I'd like you to meet a friend of mine, Rico Lupe. Rico, this is Wallace Whipkey. He owns an important gallery in New York."

Whipkey looked Rico up and down, then made a wide-eyed face at Madilyn. He ducked his chin and arched his eyebrows to his hairline and pursed his lips till they were white at the edges. Madilyn seemed pleased by his expression. Rico found it distasteful.

"I don't know how *important* it is, dear," Whipkey said.

A young man at Whipkey's elbow laughed and smiled. He was tall and angular and had reddish-brown skin and short black hair. His shoes were black and his pants were black and his shirt was a deep iridescent blue. It turned out that he laughed and smiled at most everything Whipkey said. Madilyn squeezed Rico's hand.

"Trust me, Rico," she said. "It's important."

Rico had to remind himself that they were debating the importance of Whipkey's art gallery. He knew nothing about it and did not care. He was irritated by the small man in the charcoal gray suit and his lanky companion. Whipkey turned his owlish face up at him.

"And what do you do, Señor Lupe?"

A few years back, a group of Anglo gays started coming to Rico's bar. They seemed to find the place quaint. They would look Rico up and down, as Whipkey had just done. They would stop talking abruptly when he approached their table and giggle when he turned away. He had remained aloof and eventually they started tipping badly and then they stopped coming. There were gays that came to his bar before them and still came after them, but those men acted decently and he treated them with the respect he showed all his well-behaved customers. This man he would treat like the ones who had no manners.

"I own a bar," he said, his voice cold and flat.

Madilyn squeezed his hand again, hard this time.

"He owns a fabulous bar in Los Huertos," she said.

"A bar, you say?" Whipkey purred.

"Rico makes the best margaritas in the world."

"Margaritas, you say?" Whipkey chortled.

The angular young man laughed and smiled. The small man gave his companion a happy glance, then turned his face back up at Rico.

"Well pray tell, Señor Lupe, how good are they?"

"The best," Madilyn said.

Whipkey swiveled his head in her direction.

"I wasn't asking *you*, dear. I was asking your big *friend*."

He gave Rico another up and down look, then turned back to Madilyn.

"Your opinion can scarccly bc cxpcctcd to bc objective."

Madilyn and the angular young man laughed and smiled. Whipkey tilted his face back at Rico.

"So how good are they, Señor Lupe?"

"Good enough."

"Hmm, I'll bet they're plenty good, yes. What's your secret?"

"No secret."

"No secret, you say? Remarkable."

The small man smiled. His lips were a tart little parsimonious curve.

"Well pray tell, Señor Lupe, you must mix us some."

The angular young man cackled. Madilyn gave Rico a fixed grin. Rico looked down at Whipkey through slitted eyes.

"I'm sure the caterer's bartender does a fine job," he said.

Madilyn took her hand away from his and self-consciously used it to scratch behind her ear. The small man raised his cloudy glass and his surprised eyebrows and his pointy chin.

"By all means, Señor Lupe, I'm sure he does. But you *must* mix us some of your *world famous* margaritas."

The angular young man laughed and laughed. Rico turned to Madilyn.

"Please excuse me," he said.

❖ ❖ ❖

She found him at the bar ten minutes later. He was finishing his first gin and tonic and considering a second.

"How's the little devil?" he asked.

Madilyn smiled and rolled her eyes.

"He's still talking about your 'world famous' margaritas. He sent me to find you."

Rico nodded and looked away. Madilyn put her hand on his forearm. It felt warm and soft.

"Whipkey is a very important client," she said.

He looked down at her hand. Her fingers were long and slender. Rico knew where the conversation was going and he regretted it. Madilyn squeezed his arm.

"Will you please mix him a damned margarita?"

Rico shook his head. He was still looking at her hand.

"No mix," he said.

She didn't seem to hear. She squeezed his forearm.

"Please?"

She let that single word hang for a moment.

"For me?"

Rico raised his head slowly. He stared into her pallid blue eyes. He watched her pupils dilate when he spoke.

"Did you ask me here to perform tricks for the real guests?"

She pulled her head back and let go of his arm.

"Of course not!"

Rico found her eyes again, stared back into them. Madilyn blinked a few times, then turned and left. Rico watched her go. Then he signaled the bartender and glanced at his watch.

❖ ❖ ❖

Madilyn didn't come back and Rico didn't go looking for her. At one point the crowd separated and he could see the small man in the charcoal suit and his angular companion. They spotted Rico and smiled at him, then Whipkey raised his glass in Rico's direction and the young man laughed. Rico did not respond. Whipkey turned his body slightly away and spoke to his young friend. The crowd closed again and Rico was glad he could no longer see them.

When his second drink was empty, Rico gathered a plate of food from the buffet table and picked at it while he wandered through the house. He passed through the living room and an attractive blond woman watched him over the shoulder of the man she was talking to. He returned her look, then went back to his food. He thought about pursuing the blond woman but all those games were a young man's work. Taking another lover under the nose of the one you were angry with. It made him feel sick and the food lost its appeal. He took his plate into the kitchen and put it on the counter next to the sink.

The kitchen was empty and he stood in it and looked around. It was a big good kitchen, with a gas restaurant stove and the omnipresent red brick floor and deep countertops of dark blue tile. There was an island in the middle with copper-clad pots and pans hanging from a rack above it. He had cooked her breakfast in this kitchen, French toast and coffee with cream.

A waitress came in, carrying a tray of dirty dishes. She was a stocky Navajo girl with a beautiful placid face. He nodded at her and she smiled serenely. She carried her tray to the sink and started unloading it. Rico put his hands in his pockets and wandered out into the hallway. An Anglo man and woman dressed in severe clothing all the way down to their clunky shoes were standing outside the kitchen talking in lowered voices. Their eyes followed him as he passed and their voices lowered further still.

He went to the nearest bathroom and found it occupied. He continued on into the depths of the house and found a bathroom that was empty. He turned on the light and closed the door and locked it. He examined the ceremonial facemask hanging over the toilet while he urinated. It was made of painted wood and feathers and was supposed to be frightening. To Rico anything hanging on a bathroom wall could only look sad. He flushed the toilet and washed his hands, glanced at himself in the mirror and saw a sad man with a lined face. He dried his hands and unlocked the door and turned off the light. Instead of going back the way he came, he went deeper into the house.

He stopped outside Madilyn's bedroom, a big square room back in a far corner of the sprawling old house. The lamp on the low side table next to the big low bed was turned on. All the furniture in the room was made of the same lustrous yellow pine. It glowed in the weak light from the lamp. Rico leaned on the doorframe and looked at the big bed, then went over and laid down on it. He looked up at the white-stuccoed ceiling, like he did after they made love. His eyes found the thin crack that forked like a snake's tongue and the swirl that looked like a satellite photograph of a hurricane.

He remembered that her hair was soft against his cheek and her skin was smooth and cool, like silk. He remembered the swell of her breasts against him and the hard points of her pelvis tucked against his. They were never in a hurry and they laid together well when it was over. They were gentle and playful. She laughed easily and often.

When Madilyn came to his bar, she was an attractive woman who made her intentions clear. There had been such women in the past and he had gone with many of them. But when he went to bed with Madilyn, and afterward when they lay together, it was different. They had been hungry for each other, but there had been less rush to feed that hunger because the hunger itself was good. And when it was over, he did not want to leave. He wasn't sure if there was something different with this woman or something had changed in him, and he had wanted to be with her again to find out. Now he wasn't sure what he wanted.

There was a tight feeling in his stomach and behind his eyes, but no tears came. He wondered if this would be the last woman, if he was through with women now. He did not want to be that old and indifferent, but being with yet another woman was too sad. This one had been good in a way he hadn't expected, in a way he didn't understand. He did not want to be an old bachelor who was too forlorn to even look at the young girls.

He lay in the soft light from the bedside lamp until the tightness went away. Then he went back through the house, back to the party, and stood outside on the porch.

He watched Madilyn talking with little Wallace Whipkey and his dark laughing companion. There was another man with them now, a tall fat Anglo in a linen suit. Whipkey had an index finger against his pointed chin and was looking up at this man, nodding slightly. Madilyn saw Rico and smiled and waved him over. Rico held up one finger—just a moment, it said—then he turned and went back inside. He went through the house and passed the blond woman; she gave him her look and he did not see it. He went out the front door and down the front walk and across the gravel and out the gate.

The moon had moved down the sky toward the west. He looked up at it and felt alone.

❖ ❖ ❖

His sign glowed red over Los Huertos del Rio Huérfano, the foot-high neon letters spelling *Rico's* in flowing script. He stood in his parking lot and looked at his sign, then he looked at the cars and noted the ones he recognized. When he walked inside, the owners of these cars waved and called out to him. The stereo was playing Mexican pop music and Chuy was behind the bar. Rico went across the noisy room and stood opposite his friend. Chuy studied Rico's face.

"It's over?" he said.

Rico did not respond at first, then he nodded slowly. Chuy shifted his weight to one foot and frowned up at his taller friend.

"You want me to keep working?"

Rico smiled a little and shook his head. Chuy stepped out from behind the bar and Rico took his place. Chuy sat at the bar and watched Rico glance around, checking on things, watched him reassume this role that was like a second skin.

"Go home to your wife," Rico said. "I'll be fine."

Chuy shook his head.

"Teresa will want to know what happened at that party. I'm not going anywhere till you tell me."

Rico laughed. He put both his hands on top of the bar and laughed again. Faces turned his direction, some smiling, all of them curious. Chuy was always tight-mouthed, and he had told no one but Teresa where Rico went. But they all had ideas.

"She'll be mad if you don't know," Rico said.

"You know it," Chuy answered.

Rico leaned down a little and smiled at Chuy. He lowered his voice.

"Maybe I won't tell you."

Chuy put his hands together and knitted his eyebrows.

"Por favor, señor. Have mercy."

Rico laughed again and moved off down the bar. He brought back his best tequila and held up the bottle.

"Let me make us some of my *world famous* margaritas, then I will tell you."

"World famous?" Chuy said.

Rico just laughed.

"What's so funny 'bout a margarita?" Chuy said.

Rico started making the drinks. He didn't laugh anymore.

"Nothing," he said. "Absolutely nothing at all."

❖ ❖ ❖

Rico told his friend about the little sharp-chinned man that he would not mix these good drinks for, and Chuy grunted his agreement. Rico told his friend that he was afraid Madilyn could be the last woman for him, and Chuy started to laugh.

"Rico," Chuy said, "they will not let it be so. No matter what you feel, the women will not tolerate it. You will be powerless against them."

Rico looked at his friend's laughing face and hoped he was right. They laughed together at his foolishness for a good long time. They stopped when Rico's customers needed attention. Chuy got up and cleared a table while Rico drew pitchers of beer and made drinks. Then he made two more margaritas for himself and his friend, and they talked some more about his evening at the rich Anglo lady's party. People left while they talked and people came in. They stopped their conversation to serve them and to clean up after them.

In the middle of their long talk, Rico felt eyes upon him and looked up. A young Spanish woman was watching him from a big crowded table in the middle of the room. She had delicate features in a broad strong face, luminous flashing eyes, and thick black hair that fell in a wave past her shoulders. She glanced often at Rico. She was very beautiful, and half his age if she was a day. The young man next to this young woman touched her arm. She leaned away. The young man leaned close to her and spoke into her ear—she flashed a polite smile and looked at Rico.

But Rico was busy again. And then he was talking with Chuy again, telling him more, making him laugh. Rico felt eyes upon him again, and looked across the room. The beautiful young Spanish woman stood at the door with her group of friends. She smiled at Rico, a big smile full of life and joy—then she was gone.

Rico told his friend of the young girl and Chuy roared his laughter.

"See? What did I tell you?" Chuy said when he could talk again. "They will never leave you be. Never. You are a man women will always want, even when you are very old and gray and can't get it up anymore."

Rico laughed some more, and hoped again that Chuy was right.

❖ ❖ ❖

Soon it was late and the bar was empty. The stereo was tuned to a country western station and turned down low. A deep-voiced man sang a slow song about a love he had wronged.

The two friends were done talking. Chuy sat at the bar and looked into his drink and Rico stood behind the bar and looked into his. They both looked up when tires crunched on the gravel at the road's edge and hissed slowly across the dirt parking lot. Chuy turned sideways on his stool so he could see who approached. A car appeared in the dim light outside and slowly eased up close to the door. Rico's chest tightened when he saw the interlocking rings on the car's grill.

"Is that who I think it is?" Chuy said.

A car door clicked open and chunked shut. Footsteps went around the back of the car. Rico's heart pounded and his scalp tingled.

"Time for me to go," Chuy said.

He slid off his stool and was halfway across the room when the bar door swung open. Madilyn stepped inside and stopped short when she saw Chuy. She flinched when the big door thumped shut behind her.

"Chuy," she said, "is that you?"

"In the flesh."

She swayed slightly and blinked a few times.

"Do you come here often?"

"Very often. Rico is a good friend of mine."

Madilyn blinked again.

"Oh," she said. "I didn't know."

She took an unsteady step to her left. Chuy eased past her and out the door. His footsteps sifted across the parking lot. Madilyn took a few steps forward and stopped again. She stuck a hip out, put a hand on it, and glared at Rico.

"Why did you leave?" she said.

"Why do you think?"

"I don't know what to think."

Rico put his hands on the bar and frowned at them.

"It wasn't much to ask," Madilyn said.

"It was everything to ask."

"A margarita for the little fucker? What's the big goddamn deal about a goddamn margarita for the little fucker."

"It has nothing to do with margaritas."

"It had everything to do with margaritas!"

Rico looked up and frowned at Madilyn. Her breathing was heavy and she swayed again. Rico stood up straight and crossed his arms across his chest.

"You're drunk," he said. "You shouldn't have driven like that."

"I'm not drunk. It's none of your damned business anyway."

She shifted her weight, stuck her other hip out, and put her hands on her waist. She tottered and Rico shrugged.

"Suit yourself. Just be careful."

"I think *you're* drunk."

"Maybe a little. But when I'm done, I walk away from here. No car ride home for me."

"It's a lousy stinking bar."

Rico's face clouded over.

"Say that again and I'll throw you out of here."

"Why wouldn't you make the little fucker a goddamn drink? You're a goddamn bartender."

He put his hands back on the bar and waited till the heat was gone from his throat. His voice was hard to control.

"Here, I'm a bartender. When I go to your house, when I meet your big deal important bastard friends, I'm a goddamn bar *owner*. Do you understand the difference?"

"I understand you're a fucking asshole."

Rico's eyes narrowed and his lip curled. Madilyn spun around and almost toppled over. She stomped out the door and around the back of her expensive car. Rico heard the driver's door open and smack shut. The engine roared. The tires raised a cloud of dust and spat sand and gravel as she swung around the parking lot and out into the dirt lane. The tires squealed when they caught pavement.

Rico stood where he was and listened to Madilyn's car hurtle down Los Huertos Road. He listened until the only sounds left were the ones she had disturbed. The night sounds came in the three front windows and mixed with the soft country music from the radio. The bugs chirping in the parking lot sounded like they were in the room. A few moments passed, then a coyote yipped down by the river, and the sound was so lonesome it made Rico's chest tighten again.

Rico lifted his glass and looked at the half-inch of liquid that was left in the bottom. It was just a drink. He wondered how many of them he had made in his life, how many he had made here in his bar. It was not the first time he had wondered these things and would not be the last. He tipped the glass to his lips, emptied it, then set it carefully on the bar top before him.

"Buena noche, señora," Rico said, his voice soft and gentle. "Please do not come again."

❖ ❖ ❖

It took Rico just a few minutes to close up. He rinsed the glasses he and Chuy had used, turned off the stereo, and shut all the windows. He stopped at the door and cut the lights, then pushed down the big switch for his neon sign. The hum from the sign stopped and its glow faded away. The night was dark and quiet when he stepped out into it and locked the big front door.

Rico's little adobe house stood on the far corner of the same lot as his bar. He walked under the two big cottonwoods and stepped over a dead branch one of them had dropped. He looked up through the trees and saw only stars. The lordly moon was no longer high overhead.

Rico went into his house and turned on a lamp. He put his stereo on and dialed in the same country western station he had just turned off in the bar. He peeled off his shirt and went in the bathroom and splashed water on his face and brushed his teeth. He went back through the living room and turned the lamp off and left the stereo on. He went in the bedroom and lay on his bed and listened to the soft music filtering in from the other room.

In his mind he saw the high moon that had looked down at him through the ancient cottonwoods outside Madilyn's house. He remembered how alone he had felt and some of that loneliness was with him again. Then he remembered the beautiful young woman who had smiled at him when she was leaving his bar. And he hoped for a third time that Chuy was right.

He fell asleep that way, on top of the bedspread, shirtless, but still wearing his long indigo jeans and his sharp-toed black cowboy boots.

Bargains and Dust

Wasting her vacation with her in-laws made her bitter and restless. The vast horizon and its limitless dome of sky made her feel even more confined. When her husband suggested a parentless day trip down to Mexico, she stopped resenting him just long enough to say yes.

Out on the highway, she complained about her in-laws' housekeeping, about the permanent piles of unwashed dishes, and the permeating smell of old dog and unspayed cat. Her husband nodded solemnly and silently, waited patiently until she was spent. Then he said:

"I know, I hate it just as much as you do."

And she knew he hated it much more, and that kept her quiet for a while. But her thoughts moved forward, across the border, and she couldn't help doubting this excursion would be an improvement. She started complaining about the Mexico of her TV-fed imagination, which was hot, dusty, and squalid. When she was all out of adjectives, her husband said:

"Yeah, it's all those things. But it's also a great place for bargain hunting."

That kept her quiet all the way to the border.

❖ ❖ ❖

The little Mexican town *was* hot and dusty—but not squalid. Poor, but with a dignity she had not expected. Certainly more dignity than she encountered among the poor of New York City. She stiffened her back at the thought and marched into another stall in the little open-air market, still not knowing what she was looking for, and not caring as long as it was a bargain.

She bickered for a while with a pretty Indios girl and bought a blanket she didn't need and didn't want. The Indios girl was no match. She got the blanket so cheap it was almost free. Now it was a hot scratchy thing to carry, so she found her husband and dumped it on him. He lumbered off to the car, to deposit it in the trunk.

She moved onto another vendor, and then another, but her mind kept returning to the Indios girl. She glanced back over her shoulder. The girl stood immobile, staring past the tiny, endlessly chattering old woman who ran the neighboring stall. She turned for a better look, pulled her sunglasses down and squinted over them, and realized that the girl looked like a client she had worked with back in law school.

Back in law school. Not all that long ago, but what a difference. Schlepping up to the Bronx to work for Family Services. Getting orders of protection and filing notices of delinquent child support. Ugh, what a mess. She had been such an idealistic little fool.

She pushed her sunglasses back up and gave a hot shiver in the dusty heat, then ran the back of her hand across her forehead. As if on cue, her husband trotted up carrying a pair of cold sodas. She batted her eyelashes at him, which was wasted effort since he couldn't see her eyes through the tinted lenses. She daintily took the offered can and drank deeply.

"Any more conquests?" her husband asked.

She smiled at him and tilted her head.

"Not yet."

He nodded and wandered away.

The client was a teenage mother from Guatemala. She married an American Hispanic while he was down there on business. When they returned to the States, he was laid off, took to drinking, and knocked her around. The last time she saw the client, the husband was in rehab and they had reconciled. She shook her head and wondered how the client's life worked out, if the baby was okay, and why she had ever bothered to try and help.

She found herself watching the Indios girl again, who was still ignoring the chattering old woman. She could imagine the two of them doing the same thing every day, the pretty young woman retreating into her daydreams while the crone spewed endlessly, most of her chatter probably memories as old and dusty as the God-forsaken country they lived in.

She focused all her attention on the Indios girl and really looked at her. She took off her dark glasses and squinted against the sun. Her client back in the Bronx was quite pretty, but she realized now that the Indios girl was much more than that. The Indios girl was exquisitely beautiful, with skin that glowed like fresh-roasted coffee beans and hair like strands of black silk.

The bitterness she had left at her in-laws came seeping back. She returned her sunglasses to her face, turned to the little molasses-colored man who ran the stall she was standing in, and practically stole his nicest piece, a hand-painted pitcher showing a pale sandy rose against a background of robin's egg blue.

He wanted thirty dollars for it. She put fifteen in his hand, picked up the pitcher, and walked away. His eyes went back and forth between her departing form and the two bills in his open hand. He tried to speak, but could not shape the words. When she was out of easy earshot, he counted the money twice, then spat in her direction.

❖ ❖ ❖

She didn't really want the bracelet. Hammered silver wasn't her taste. She was a gold-and-diamonds girl. She didn't know anyone whose taste it was, so she couldn't make a gift of it. But it was the best piece of workmanship she had seen all day, and its quality held her. She turned it over in her hands more than a few times, then finally tried it on.

It didn't fit. Her wrists had grown too fat. She realized with embarrassment that other things didn't fit anymore, and she yanked her skirt down violently. She glared up at the shopkeeper, just in case he was watching. He wasn't.

So she watched him for a while. He was moving among his merchandise, cleaning and straightening up. His right leg was caved in and he had a horrible scooped-out limp. She wondered if it was a birth defect or an accident. If it was an accident, she could have gotten him a hell of a settlement back in New York. The poor little wetback wouldn't be hustling trinkets on some dusty side street.

He suddenly spun around and frowned at her. She blushed and looked away, then went back to fondling the bracelet. A moment or two passed.

"Señora, you like?"

She looked up. He was standing next to her. She turned toward him, then took a step back.

"How much?"

"Thirty-five dollars."

She snorted, then fondled the bracelet some more.

"I'll give you ten."

He looked at her warily.

"No, señora. That is too little."

"Well, how much then?"

He watched her some more.

"Twenty-five dollars."

She snorted again. She shook her head violently. She was spinning the bracelet around in her hands.

"Twelve," she said.

He shrugged and walked away.

She tried the bracelet on again. It still didn't fit and she knew it never would. She glanced over at the Indios girl, who looked both utterly feminine and entirely impervious. The desert breeze fanned her obsidian hair, and the crone's chatter sounded like dim, tinkling piano music.

In her mind, she saw the bracelet slipping easily onto the girl's wrist and how stunning it would look against her dark skin. She glared down at it, then sneered at her pale fat bulging out around the intricately worked silver. She snatched it off her arm and was tempted to throw it back onto the display table.

But she didn't. She resumed her fondling, turning the bracelet over and over in her hands. After a minute or two, the limping Mexican came back to her.

"Twenty dollars."

"Twelve."

Hints of anger flashed across the vendor's face, but he said nothing. She tried to stare him down, but she couldn't find the focus of his black eyes, and he couldn't see hers through the dark lenses.

Her husband appeared. He glanced around the stall, saw the bracelet in her hand, looked at the vendor, and sighed.

"Ready to go?" he asked his wife.

She did not answer. She began spinning the bracelet again. Moments came and went. Her husband sighed again.

"Eighteen dollars," the Mexican said.

"Twelve," she repeated.

The vendor threw up his hands and walked around in a little circle. More lethargic moments passed through the dust and heat. Her husband sighed for a third time.

"Come on, honey. Pay the man his price or forget it."

"No!" she screeched.

Her husband frowned at her dispassionately, then shrugged.

"Suit yourself," he said, and wandered away.

She glared at the vendor. She took a step toward him and he backed away.

"Fifteen dollars," she hissed, "and not one goddamn penny more."

❖ ❖ ❖

It was late on a Sunday night when they got back to New York. She didn't unpack till Monday evening after work. She unfolded the blanket and decided it was an ugly thing, so she stuffed it into the closet in the guest room. The pitcher looked a little sad, even after she washed off the dust, but it was a poetic kind of melancholy, so she gave it a prominent place on a shelf in the kitchen.

She almost missed the bracelet. It had slipped down to the bottom of her bag. She didn't notice it rattling around in there until she was jamming the bag back into its customary place on the shelf in the hall closet.

She stood in the hallway and unwrapped it. The silver caught a little of the dim light and gave a strange yellowish glint. She squinted at it a bit, then moved into the kitchen and tried the light in there. The bracelet glowed. She turned it over in her hands and examined the workmanship. Her face was blank and impassive. Once or twice she almost smiled.

She didn't bother to try it on again. She spent a few more minutes fondling the metal and almost smiling, then she clomped upstairs to her bedroom. She dropped the intricately worked silver into the bottom drawer of her dresser, gave it her odd little almost-smile one last time, then slammed the drawer so hard the whole wall shook.

The Ugly Wife

When he first saw her, as she turned on the landing below his apartment door, Tim froze, stared, and drew in his breath. Josephine Flaum was shockingly ugly. She was large and trunk shaped, with no figure to her form, no bust or hips. Her shoulders were rounded in a fixed slouch that angled her neck and thrust her head forward. Her hair was thin and lank, a shineless brown curtain falling just below her heavy jaw. Her face was long and ashen, with close-set dishwater eyes, a thick pulpy nose, and thin purple-gray lips.

Tim forced a smile, hoped it wasn't a grimace, and was shocked again when he saw her response to his reaction: a knowing look, a sly expression that came and went. He knew in that instant Josephine had found power in her ugliness—and it scared him. He had never encountered the like of it before.

Right behind Josephine, eyes wide and grinning like a fool, was her husband, Martin Flaum. The contrast couldn't have been more pronounced: Martin was preposterously handsome, tall and broad-shouldered, with glowing blond hair, a cleft chin, and shining blue eyes. His high cheeks were ruddy from the first chill of fall, and his big white teeth glistened. Women stared at Martin with dewy eyes and smiled vacantly when he spoke. Tim had assumed Martin was married to a beauty—not the ugliest wife he had ever seen. What went wrong on the way to the altar?

Tim met Martin just two weeks before, when Martin was hired by Tim's employers. Over lunch later that day, Tim learned the Flaums were new in town, and were staying with relatives way up in Rhinebeck while they looked for an apartment in the city. Offhandedly, Tim offered to give Martin a tour of his Brooklyn neighborhood. He regretted it mildly when Martin accepted, and regretted it massively now. He had already experienced revulsion, guilt, and fear—and the visit was only a few seconds old.

"Hello!" Tim called out too loudly.

"Hello!" Martin bellowed back.

The ugly wife mounted the last few steps and stood before Tim, hand outstretched, a thin smile draped across her bruised-looking lips.

"I'm Jo Flaum," she said.

He took her hand. It was limp and damp. He shook it twice and dropped it. He did not wipe his hand on his pants, but it did occur to him.

"Tim Harret. Welcome to Brooklyn!" he said, too loudly again.

Almost at the end of her nose, just off to one side of the tip—it seemed like too much, but there it was, he couldn't ignore it—was a protruding wart. At least there weren't any hairs growing out of it. Tim forced his gaze up and met Josephine's eyes. She had seen where he was looking, but instead of the anger or embarrassment he expected, there was contained, expectant glee. Tim felt a cold tingle on his spine as he looked away. He wondered if the wart was hairless because she had trimmed it, which led to his noticing that Josephine was immaculately groomed and dressed. He had rarely seen anyone so ugly, and had never seen anyone half as ugly who was so carefully put together. Tim was dumbfounded.

"Well!" Martin hollered, "Aren't you going to invite us in?"

Tim did, mumbled and clumsily, and they accepted.

❖ ❖ ❖

But they didn't stay long. He gave them the nickel tour of his apartment, offered them a drink, and when they declined, suggested they get started on the neighborhood. He didn't want to be trapped inside with the Flaums for a moment longer. His eyes kept wandering to her wart, or her jutting neck, or some other grotesquerie, and Jo or Martin's eyes would invariably find his when he managed to draw his gaze from whatever feature had claimed it. Josephine would give him that pleased, patient look, and his skin would crawl. Martin would grin like a crazy man, and Tim's stomach would turn.

They walked down Henry Street, through Cobble Hill to Carroll Gardens. Tim prattled on as they went, pointing out shops and restaurants he was familiar with, mentioning anything on which he could comment. He offered what little local lore he knew, most of it mob-related. They went as far as Third Street, then came back up on Court. He couldn't help noticing that every third or fourth passerby gave Josephine Flaum a quick shocked look or stared at her outright. On the streets of New York City, reactions from passers-by are hard won. Jo was a sensation.

Tim hoped he could avoid having a meal with the Flaums, but like a vindictive mind reader, that was exactly what Josephine suggested. Martin chimed in that he was starving, they hadn't had time for much of a breakfast. So Tim was trapped.

Jo suggested Chinese food, so they went to Wong's, on Montague Street, where Tim was a regular. His favorite waiter met them at the door, a tall impassive Indonesian with a moon face. He was older than the rest of the wait staff, probably around fifty. Tim was relieved that he didn't register any reaction to Josephine's appearance.

From the moment they entered, Jo took charge. She picked the table they sat at, decided who took which chair, then vocally perused the menu. She peppered the waiter with questions, most of which seemed designed to advertise her knowledge of Chinese cooking. When the ordering was done, she launched into a discourse on art and multiculturalism, repeatedly punctuated by rhetorical questions. Tim found himself nodding frequently. Martin nodded almost constantly. The appetizers came and went. They were about five minutes into the main course when Tim realized how completely Jo Flaum was in control. She was shepherding the conversation, picking the topics and stringing them together, doing most of the talking, which she peppered with her beloved rhetorical questions that begged politically correct answers. Tim couldn't help thinking Josephine would make an excellent politician if she wasn't so incredibly ugly.

Tim found himself irritated by her domination and painfully bored with her tedious liberalista subjects and their tired foregone conclusions. He stopped waiting for her to stop and started considering his options—and decided it was best to let Jo have her way. Breaking the conversation away from her careful management would be a challenge and an insult. And what would he offer in substitute? How could he hope to compete with her ceaseless chatter? He'd already talked himself out on the streets of Brooklyn. But most of all, he already felt guilty for the revulsion her appearance caused him. Hurting her also would be too much for his strained conscience to bear. So he put a thoughtful look back on his face and nodded some more.

Josephine Flaum worked in an art gallery in Soho. She was an assistant manager, or an assistant to the manager, or some sort of assistant something. She name-dropped effortlessly. Unfortunately, the names she dropped meant nothing to Tim. Occasionally Martin would offer his fool's grin, so Tim would smile slightly. Sometimes he pinched the tender skin on the inside of his forearm. His irritation flared when he found himself nodding agreement to things he didn't really agree with.

Later, Tim would particularly regret nodding along to Jo's assertion that Native Americans had every right to demonize Christopher Columbus. By her reasoning—or more accurately, Tim thought, by the line of reasoning Jo had adopted—Columbus was accountable for all the oppression and exploitation the native peoples had suffered in his wake. Tim had read about the horrors Columbus and his men had perpetrated, but holding the iconic explorer responsible for all of the genocide in the Americas seemed a bit much to Tim at the time, and more so later. His mother was half Italian and Columbus was a hero on that side of the family. Despite his personal opinion that Columbus was the worst type of man, Tim felt like a traitor for not defending him.

The Flaums let Tim get the check. In fact, they seemed to expect it. When the waiter returned with Tim's credit card and receipt, Jo asked one last question about the food, something about one of the sauces. A look flashed across the waiter's face and Tim knew the impassive Indonesian didn't like Jo Flaum. Tim and the waiter had a rapport, and Tim considered the older man to be his superior in matters of human wisdom. His realization that this man he respected already disliked Josephine forced another: Tim realized that he disliked Josephine also, and he only felt guilty about it because Josephine was ugly. If she was pretty or plain—or even just not so *very* ugly—he would have been perfectly comfortable disliking her.

The waiter left. Tim looked across the table at the Flaums. Jo was frowning slightly, as if deep in thought about the sauce. Martin flashed his idiot's grin. Tim wanted to jump up and run out of the restaurant, out into the honesty of the brutal Brooklyn streets.

❖ ❖ ❖

Tim and Martin shared a small office in the core of a tall glass tower a few blocks from Wall Street.

They were computer programmers, employed by a fast-growing consulting firm to service the technological needs of huge financial conglomerates. Tim tried to get along with his new coworker, but after a month at close quarters, he knew Martin Flaum to be conceited, a bad listener, and a devout contrarian. Almost every opinion or suggestion Tim offered was doubted or rebuked. Even simple greetings were often challenged; if Martin found the weather to be disagreeable, saying "good morning" invited a diatribe. Their rare moments of harmony just served to emphasize the general discord.

A few weeks after the Flaums visited Brooklyn, while half-listening to Martin tear apart a movie Tim had liked, Tim found himself wondering if Martin married Josephine just to prove he was a freethinking man. No conventions of attractiveness for Martin Flaum—his woman was both hideous *and* unbearable. It seemed rather self-flagellating for the otherwise self-congratulatory and self-indulgent Martin, but Tim couldn't entirely reject the theory—mostly because it was the only theory he had.

So after six weeks of sharing that small office with no windows, it was with great relief that Tim learned that his petition to work at home had finally been approved. His new working arrangement would coincide with the start of a new project. The project was staffed with two programmers: Tim would be the project's lead programmer—and his only underling would be Martin.

Tim managed to fake some enthusiasm when Martin said he was looking forward to working together on this new project. Tim struggled to hide his disappointment when Martin announced that the

Flaums had rented an apartment just five blocks from Tim's—he needn't have tried, since Martin was too deep in self-congratulation for Tim's displeasure to register. Tim had to refrain from kicking himself when Martin announced that he would also be working at home—so they could easily meet whenever they needed.

And then a moment arrived that Tim had once dreaded and thought was safely dodged.

"We should get together sometime," Martin said. "Have a few beers."

"Sure," Tim said.

"Jo would love to get together again."

"Great."

For almost a week, Tim lived in fear of this social obligation finally being called down upon him. He froze whenever the phone rang. Finally, on the following Monday afternoon, after the weekly staff meeting at the consulting firm's headquarters (on lower Broadway, just south of Liberty Street), Martin approached Tim as he was pulling on his coat. *Here it comes*, Tim thought, and immediately felt hot and flushed.

But Martin only wanted to discuss their new project. After that, Tim felt the dreaded event had been successfully dodged once and for always. He was correct: the threatened social occasion never came to pass.

❖ ❖ ❖

Tim and Martin quickly settled into a new work routine: once or twice a week, one of them would walk over to the other's apartment, where they would exchange files and discuss the project's progress and direction. These discussions usually started with Tim presenting his ideas for what should be done next and how. Martin consistently debated two-thirds of Tim's thinking and was skeptical or silent in response to the rest. Martin's suggestions were infrequent, seldom practical, and rarely significant.

When a new problem presented itself that did not have an obvious solution, Tim at first solicited Martin's input in analyzing the issue. He quickly learned that was a mistake. When so prompted, Martin delighted in blowing problems up to hopelessly unsolvable proportions. There was rarely any substantive thinking behind these discourses, and when there was, Martin volunteered it enthusiastically. So Tim became comfortable with an autocratic approach, analyzing problems on his own and dictating how they should be solved, since this was both more efficient *and* didn't preclude any valid input. Martin didn't seem to mind. He grumbled a little now and then, but his mood remained overtly cheerful.

Working with Martin presented another dilemma that was harder for Tim to resolve: which apartment he preferred for their meetings. Going to the Flaums' meant he could leave whenever he wanted. When Martin came over, getting rid of him wasn't always easy. But the Flaums' apartment was not pleasant—the ceiling was low, the light bad, and the decor incongruously Southwestern. Josephine had hand-painted their furniture in a busy assortment of loud pastels, which only accented the apartment's general gloom. Their few rooms were in the dank basement of a decrepit brownstone, with sole access to an overgrown backyard. Martin and Jo had selected it because they had two large dogs—or so Martin said.

Tim never met the dogs. He entered into the living room, which was in the middle of the apartment, and the dogs were always locked up in the front room. He could hear them moving around, scraping against walls and doors and furniture, but they never barked or whined. He could smell something animal, but only occasionally, and in powerful bursts.

Walking home from his third visit to the Flaums' apartment, Tim realized it was the hidden dogs that particularly disturbed him. On his first visit, Tim had mentioned that he would like to meet the dogs—initially just to be polite, but as he said it, he felt a budding curiosity. In retrospect, Martin's response seemed prepared but not practiced—it was delivered quickly and loudly, but haltingly, as if he was searching for certain phrases. His answer was also overlong and redundant.

Martin firmly dismissed any introduction to the dogs. He said they were too excitable, that getting them back into the front room would be too difficult, and that doing so would take far too much time. Then he repeated that they were too excitable, and that rounding them up again would take up too much time. His voice trailed off when he got back around to how hard it would be to close them up again. Tim had already stopped listening to Martin's answer and was trying to hear the dogs.

So when Tim visited, the dogs lurked, emitting their odd scraping sounds. Tim found himself wondering if they were actually dogs at all. *They could be goats for all I know—awfully quiet for excitable dogs*, he found himself thinking as he made his way up Henry Street, feeling carefree and lightheaded after escaping the Flaums' gloom.

❖ ❖ ❖

On a Tuesday in October, Martin came by Tim's apartment after lunch. For the second time, the unsavory appearance of a Flaum shocked Tim when he opened his apartment door. Seemingly overnight, the tall manly Nordic stud had lost hair and sprouted a beer gut. Martin was unshaven and greasy looking. Tim held the door open and stepped aside. When Martin passed, Tim smelled sweat and unwashed feet. He followed Martin down the apartment's hall and couldn't help noticing that the other man's khakis were rather tight in the ass, and that he waddled slightly. *When did that happen?* Tim thought. *He didn't look like that last week.*

The meeting was pointless. Martin hadn't completed the work Tim assigned and offered nothing but ill-conceived excuses and dismissive cynicism. He displayed no embarrassment at his appearance or for his performance—and to Tim's dismay, made no move to leave, and would not shut up. Martin talked incessantly, starting new and entirely unrelated topics with abandon. He talked about TV shows and sports and music and city politics. Tim fought his encroaching sympathy. The man was pathetic, and despite himself, Tim felt bad.

Eventually Martin did stop talking, and then the silence was thick. After a long moment, he glanced at his watch, found it wasn't working, shrugged, then grunted. He asked the time and Tim told him it was a quarter of two. Martin grunted again, stood up, and said he had to walk the dogs. Tim saw him to the door but could think of nothing to say.

An hour passed. Tim did some work, then made a cup of coffee and took it into the living room. He stood before one of the tall windows, sipping from his mug and watching the street below. He lived on the second floor and the window offered a nice view up Henry Street. It was a bright breezy autumn day, the kind that is New York's best, and Tim wanted to go for a nice long walk over the Brooklyn Bridge to Chinatown. He craved some dumplings and a big plate of lo mein.

But his workload wouldn't allow it, and that was Martin's fault. The big now-going-to-seed hunk was useless. He stalled and made excuses and said certain things couldn't be done—so Tim took those things away from him and proved Martin wrong. Tim was mulling this over, his resentment growing by the moment, when he saw Josephine Flaum sauntering down Henry Street.

She was talking with animation to a tall wiry man, a dark-haired bearded fellow with glasses. Tim saw her turn her head, saw her lips move, and just knew that she was posing one of her beloved rhetorical questions. And then Tim looked at her companion, and it hit him, square and hard: she was having an affair with this guy. It was almost as shocking as her unexpected ugliness. How on earth did she do it? And this guy was handsome too!

The two lovers continued toward Tim's window, Josephine talking, the bearded man nodding. At the precise moment that Tim's conviction about their relationship started to slip, Jo took the man's arm and beamed up into his face. The man bent down and gave her a quick furtive kiss.

"Holy shit," Tim said.

❖ ❖ ❖

Tim began avoiding Martin. He said he was too busy to meet. They exchanged files and ideas by email instead of conversation and diskette. Martin's productivity continued to deteriorate, which directly increased Tim's workload, so his lies about being too busy quickly became true.

Tim reported Martin's failings to his employers. When the project was completed, they immediately canceled Martin's contract. Tim had suspected he worked for sharks but the confirmation was shocking. Whatever happened to a second chance?

Over the next few weeks, Tim saw Martin on the street twice and managed to avoid being seen himself. Martin grew fatter, had less and less hair, and was perpetually unshaven. It was the rapid balding that Tim found most disturbing. Martin's hair seemed to be falling like snow. Tim never saw either Flaum walking the purported dogs. He couldn't help envisioning that cramped little backyard behind their apartment as fouled beyond comprehension. Tim wondered if the Flaums would get evicted.

The last time he saw Martin, Tim was walking up Clinton Street to the subway, going into Manhattan for the weekly staff meeting. He had a report to deliver and was lost in thought, walking with his head down, eyes on the concrete sidewalk. About two blocks from the subway entrance, Tim felt a presence and looked up. There was Martin, straight ahead, grinning wildly and waddling rapidly, closing on Tim fast.

Tim froze momentarily, then dove across the street in front of a taxi. The driver blasted his horn and cursed Tim in Arabic. When the honking ceased, Tim could hear hysterical laughter. He looked across the street and Martin was pointing at him, his balding head thrown back, laughing like a lunatic.

After this unfortunate encounter, Tim walked the streets like a frightened cat. His eyes roamed ahead and to the sides as he scurried along. He made frequent and abrupt stops to spin around and peer behind him. He imagined encounters that ended in violence. At first this felt like rank paranoia, but it did not take long for Tim to conclude that his fear of Martin was legitimate. This conviction grew from his frequent review of the following facts: while working together, their relationship had gone from passable to impossible; then Tim had gotten Martin fired, which Martin would definitely deduce; meanwhile, Martin's appearance and behavior had grown strange and were getting stranger; and finally, Martin's ugly wife was cheating on him. It was entirely possible, given his irrational state, that Martin would blame Tim for his descent. Who knew what Martin might do if suddenly confronted by Tim's presence on a street corner? Maybe next time he wouldn't just laugh.

One night, Tim dreamt that he bumped into Martin outside a pizzeria on Court Street. Martin was bloated and stinking but still full of vigor. He hit Tim over the head and dragged him home to his subterranean apartment, where he fed Tim's corpse to those mysterious dogs. They looked like a cross between pit bulls and mountain goats, and they never barked or growled or vocalized in any way. They just gobbled Tim up in enormous bites. When the dream ended, Tim woke up completely and abruptly. He put the light on and looked at the clock, then put the light out and lay awake in the dark. He watched the ceiling and listened to distant sirens and cursed himself for ever inviting the Flaums to Brooklyn.

❖ ❖ ❖

Months passed. Tim's vigilance when out on the streets lost its hysteria but did not disappear—he stopped twitching like a scalded rat and simply became more observant. He was surprised to note how often people he knew did not notice him, and the multitude of things he had overlooked on the streets that he thought he knew: faded signs painted on brick walls, religious icons perched in high windows, old insurance medallions bolted to the fronts of buildings. His new habits of observation never found Martin, but they did locate Martin's wife—if the Flaums were still married by then.

It was early afternoon on a clear cold Saturday at the tail end of winter. Tim was approaching the corner of Clinton Street and Atlantic Avenue, heading toward the Brooklyn Bridge and eventually Chinatown. He was on the east side of the street, coming up on the southeast corner of the intersection. Josephine Flaum was on the far corner, the northwest one, talking on a pay phone. Her behavior was jumpy. She appeared alarmed. She turned this way and that, continuously scanning the crowd, never leaving her back in one direction for more than a few seconds. She gesticulated sharply with her free hand and shouted into the receiver. She was apparently extremely agitated and very cross with whom she conversed.

Tim's entire attention locked onto Jo Flaum. He didn't see the light change, just started walking when everyone else did. He kept his eyes on her as he crossed the street, then lost her as he approached the curb. He almost bumped into an old woman, glanced to the pavement as he stepped across the gutter to the sidewalk, then found his view blocked by the corner light post and his path by a tight throng of pedestrians. When he skirted these obstacles, Josephine Flaum was gone.

He spun around wildly, searching the streets in every direction. She was nowhere to be seen. Her disappearance was so complete and inexplicable that when he turned back toward the pay phone, he expected to see her standing there. She was not—and she had lacked the time or concern to hang up the receiver. It dangled violently, hopping on its cord in the bitter wind. His eyes zeroed in on it and its erratic twisting motion became sinister and malevolent. A hot chill started in his heels and burnt a path to his scalp.

"Holy shit," Tim said.

Tim continued to Chinatown and had his habitual dumplings and lo mein. Every few minutes, the sensations of Jo Flaum's disappearance—or abduction?—replayed in his mind. When the feelings came, he was paralyzed by them, then warmly relieved when the sensations passed. He drained his pot of tea and flagged down a waiter for another.

Tim ran a few errands after his lunch and returned home in the early evening. He forced himself to try the Flaums' phone number and found it disconnected. When it was completely dark, he went for a walk, and on his third pass by the Flaums' building, he worked up the nerve to step into the vestibule. There was a new name on the mailbox for the basement apartment. Tim was surprised by his deep sense of relief. He went back outside and stood on the sidewalk. Standing under the yellow streetlights, listening to the muted sound of traffic from the BQE, he considered the possibility that one or both of the Flaums had remained in the neighborhood, which New Yorkers often do when their relationships disintegrate. But something told Tim the Flaums were gone for good. And if they were gone for good, then whatever had happened to Josephine earlier that day was somehow not his problem. Tim turned and went home.

The Flaums had lived on a nice block. Tim had walked it frequently before they moved in. He resumed doing so now that they had left. The block's association with Martin and Josephine quickly faded. He often passed their building without noticing it, without remembering Martin Flaum, his unseen dogs, and his ugly and unfaithful wife.

But another association remained powerful and resolute—Tim couldn't pass the pay phone at the corner of Atlantic and Clinton without recalling the dangling receiver, swinging like a hanged man in the middle of the Saturday crowds. That dirty banged-up public telephone became an icon for Tim Harret, emblematic of the anonymous grief going on all around him. He could not look at it without a chill and a shudder, even in the middle of a broiling summer day.

❖ ❖ ❖

A year passed and winter came again. It was a Sunday in late March. Tim was reading the *Times*, eating a second bagel, and procrastinating his laundry. It was fifteen degrees outside and windy. To do the laundry required hauling it several blocks to the laundromat.

Tim was reading the wedding announcements—not his usual fare. He stumbled upon them when the newspaper slipped from his hands and scattered across the floor. In the past, before the Flaums entered his life and even while they were first in it, he would have ignored whatever the paper presented him when he bent to pick it up. He would have irritably continued his pursuit of the section he was turning to, which in this case was the want ads. But the habits of observation that arose from his dread of Martin had stimulated interest in things previously overlooked. So now the photographs of beaming couples and the earnest text describing their ceremonies struck him as fascinating.

He read about an ambassador's daughter marrying the scion of an investment banking family in St. Patrick's Cathedral. Then he read about a television anchorwoman and a sports entrepreneur wedding in a private home out in the Hamptons. Next were two professors, he of linguistics at Columbia and she of physics at NYU, joined in Temple Emanu-El. Tim skimmed a few—one that took place in Boca Raton, another in Short Hills, a third in Detroit. Then he stopped at the next announcement and stared.

It was a small photo, but how many women are that ugly? Her name was Josephine Kroenistz now. Tim studied the groom for several minutes, trying to decide if shaving could change a man's appearance so drastically. He concluded it could not. Whoever he was, the ugly wife had not married the bearded man that Tim had seen kissing her on Henry Street. But true to form, her new husband was quite handsome. Wide cheekbones, deep-set brooding eyes. Not as dark as the bearded man or as light as Martin, as best Tim could tell from the grainy black-and-white photo.

He read the accompanying text and learned that the groom was an artist from Denmark with an international reputation. His parents were a prominent surgeon and a human rights lawyer. Both of his grandfathers were active in the resistance during WWII. The couple met when he had a show at the gallery where Josephine was Assistant Manager.

Jo was essentially nobody. Her father sold cars in Florida and her mother was a housewife in Spokane. Her grandparents were apparently not worth mentioning.

Tim looked at the photo again. Time had not tempered Josephine's ugliness. If anything, she had become even more grotesque. Why would a world-famous artist marry a hideous woman? Weren't they supposed to wed gorgeous creatures that came to their studios half-starved and posed naked for pennies? The thought of a naked Jo posing for her portrait gave Tim a shiver.

"How on earth does she do it?" Tim asked.

He put down the paper and looked out a tall window. Clouds huddled against a steely sky, wind rattled the old windows, and a cold gust swept through the room. A siren went down Atlantic Avenue.

Voices came from the apartment above. It had recently been rented by an attractive couple that Tim assumed were newlyweds. The man called out from above Tim's head and the woman's laughter answered from down the hall. Footsteps approached and stopped, furniture creaked, the man spoke again, not so loudly now, and the woman laughed again, this time right over Tim. The couple talked and Tim listened to their muffled voices while he looked around his Spartan bachelor quarters.

When the voices above stopped, Tim remembered Josephine Flaum turning on the landing beneath his apartment door, looking up at him with her sly knowing expression. He saw her being kissed by the bearded man on the street outside his apartment. He heard Martin's diabolical laughter echoing down the Brooklyn blocks. He saw the once-studly fat man standing on the sidewalk across the street—head back, arm outstretched, pointing.

Tim Harret found the want ads he had been looking for. It was time to find a new apartment. It was time to find a new neighborhood. It was time to find a new job. It might be time to begin a new career. It was past time to begin a new life.

The Bully Bleeder

Georgie was a creepy kid. He was smart for his age but he wasted it being clever. He'd ask you a trick question, hound you till you admitted you were stumped, then tell you the answer and point out how smart that proved he was.

He was lanky and real tall for eleven. He had a wide flat face and gray-blond hair that was a little darker than his skin. He was also a hemophiliac. That was what he was most known for around the apartment complex, being a bleeder. There weren't any other bleeders. Georgie was the first I'd ever met and the same with the other kids.

He talked about it all the time. Georgie bragged about being a bleeder.

"I have to go to the hospital in a month," he'd say.

He'd butt right into the middle of a conversation, like anybody cared. We all knew his mother had to take him to some hospital in Philadelphia for some kind of blood treatment every four months, 'cause he always talked about it.

"I have to go to the hospital next week," he'd say. "I have to get blood treatment or I might bleed to death."

Like we'd all just met him and didn't know. And when he'd been to the hospital and came back, he'd talk about that.

"I had to go the hospital last week," he'd say. "For blood treatment. If I don't get it I could bleed to death from a little scratch."

If he wasn't looking, we'd all start walking away. Sometimes we got pretty far before he noticed. We didn't bother if he was looking 'cause he'd just follow us and keep talking.

Georgie liked to pick on kids that were smaller than him, and that was a lot of kids 'cause he was big. He would push the smaller kids around and say—

"You can't push me back 'cause I'm a bleeder. If you cut me, I might bleed to death."

And they'd take it. He would push them around till they fell down. Me and the other bigger kids gave him hell for it, but he didn't stop. We wanted to beat him up so bad. He was such a jerk. He went after every kid that was smaller and weaker. Or at least appeared weaker, and that's not something you can always judge so well by looks. Georgie learned that the hard way and had it coming.

We all went to Georgie's eleventh birthday party 'cause our parents made us. No one wanted to go. We'd been to his place before and knew the drill. But all the parents felt sorry for him and his mother, so we had to go.

His dad wasn't around. His mother said it was because Georgie was a bleeder and his dad had no guts. Georgie's mom was tall and skinny like him. They looked almost exactly alike, except she dyed her hair yellow. She smoked like a chimney.

There wasn't much furniture at Georgie's so at his party I had to eat on the floor. He had this nasty Siamese cat that loved potato chips, and of course his mom always served them. It wasn't cross-eyed like other Siamese, it had killer eyes. If it got next to your plate it would sit there and eat until all your chips were gone. If you tried to stop it, the little bastard would rip your hand to shreds. So the best strategy was to keep tossing it chips so it'd stay away, and that's what I did. When the chips were all gone, it came over and inspected my plate, then hissed at me and left. I thought the cat was done with me. I should have known better.

After we'd eaten Georgie's cake, I found a place on the couch and sat down. Soon as I did, his damned cat jumped in my lap, tucked its legs under, closed its eyes and started purring real loud. I tried to pet it and it spun its head around, bit my finger and drew blood. I waited a minute and tried to push it off, but it shredded the soft skin on the inside of my arm. So I sat there with the furry terror purring on my lap and wondered how come Georgie was still alive with this bloodthirsty little shit living in his house.

So that's what Georgie was like, and what his deal was. I guess you know already he's the bad guy in this story. The problem is, the good guy's not much better.

Alan was a creepy kid too. He was pretty smart too, but not clever like Georgie. He didn't hit you over the head with it, he just slowly bored you to death. He didn't know how to just talk. He'd come up with some weird comment about space rocket propulsion systems when you were talking about baseball. Or he'd talk about baseball when you were talking about girls. Or about girls when it was rockets. He couldn't ever get it right. And he talked real loud, we were always yelling at him to stop yelling at us.

He was older than the rest of us, a year older than me. So he got horny before we did. Some people are just really gross when they're horny. He talked about girls' bodies and what he wanted to do with them in a way I just didn't like. He showed us one of his dad's *Playboys* once, and the centerfold had really big boobs. Alan liked that a lot. He said this weird thing.

"I wish I had a big breast," he said. "Just one breast. Unattached. I'd keep it in my room and play with it."

It wasn't just the words, it was how he said it. Like he was so desperate, and that one big boob would be the greatest thing. I looked him in the face and felt like I wanted to throw up.

He was such an ugly kid. He was tiny and had a frog face and that thing where your upper lip is split at birth and they sew it back together. It looked like the guy who did his used a knitting needle. Then he was in a fire when he was small and it burnt one side of his face, melted his ear off. He had surgery about once a year to rebuild things but it never seemed to get any better. There was this little piece of skin that connected one nostril to his cheek. That was the grossest thing of all.

The fire he was in killed his mother. His dad wasn't around much, and he brought women home when he was. His dad was really handsome. When he brought the chicks home he would send Alan outside, if he couldn't dump the kid at his grandparents. His grandparents bought him stuff and brought him back as quick as they could. He always came back from there with lots of new toys, but he always came back sooner than he was supposed to.

One night my mom sent me out with the trash when it was late. I think it was about 10:30 or 10:45. My building was next to Alan's and up a short hill. I saw him sitting on the back steps of his building. There was a light over the door and he was sitting under it, reading a book. I felt bad for him but I made sure he didn't see me. I didn't like Alan. Nobody did.

Georgie especially liked to push Alan around 'cause he was two years older than Georgie. He liked to taunt Alan about being so little and being left back in school. Alan was in the hospital for a whole year after the fire, but Georgie didn't care. You'd think he'd have some sympathy, being a bleeder, but he didn't. None at all.

One day we were all hanging around after school and Georgie started in. He pushed Alan off a step and Alan fell in the grass. He got up and pointed at Georgie.

"You better stop doing that," Alan said.

"Yeah? Who's gonna stop me?"

I told Georgie he was being a jerk and he acted like he didn't hear. He always did that. He didn't dare push me 'cause he knew I'd cream him. But he knew I didn't dare push him first. Pick a fight with Georgie and all the parents in the apartment complex would be on your ass.

"If you do that again," Alan said, "I might push you back."

Georgie laughed at him.

"You *might* push me back."

"That's right," Alan said. "I'm getting really sick of it. Next time, or maybe the time after that, I might lose my temper. I might get mad and push you back."

Georgie tried to look cool, but his eyes got squirrelly. He saw a little black girl go by on a bicycle and he yelled something and ran off after her. She put her head down and rode away fast.

"He better watch it," Alan said. "I've had about all I can take."

I could feel Alan looking at me, wanting to make contact. He was always so hungry for it, always looking right at you. I felt bad for the guy, but just looking at him made my stomach turn over. So I nodded and kept my face turned.

"Yeah," I said, "he'd better watch it."

"That's right," Alan said. "Damn straight."

Alan must have made an impression 'cause Georgie left him alone for a while.

❖ ❖ ❖

The trouble happened about two weeks before school started. We were kicking a ball around in the parking lot between F building and G building. The blacktop was really potholed, but there wasn't any better place to do it. It was me and Alan and this black kid named Dan who never said anything. He lived in G building. Almost everyone in G building was black.

There were two little girls off to one side playing on a little patch of grass. Georgie came around the corner of F building and they yelled at him.

"Georgie's a bleeder, Georgie's a bleeder!"

They were so little even he couldn't get away with pushing them, so he ignored them and came over to play with us. The ball came his direction and he kicked it past Alan.

"Run, ya little squirt!" he yelled.

Alan ran after it. It went up on the back porch of F building. Alan went up the two concrete steps and kicked it back at Georgie and hit him in the head.

"Hey, watch it!" Georgie yelled. "That almost hit my nose! A nosebleed could kill me."

"It wasn't intentional," Alan said.

He was still standing up on the porch.

"I could bleed to death."

"I know. You say that all the time."

Georgie started toward Alan.

"What?"

"You say that all the time. If a nosebleed could kill you, maybe you shouldn't play."

Georgie went up the two steps. I yelled at him to stop it and he ignored me like he always did.

"I'll play if I want to."

"Then you might get killed."

"Yeah?"

They started circling each other. Georgie pushed Alan.

"Don't do that, Georgie."

Georgie pushed.

"If you do that one more time, I'm going to push you back."

Georgie pushed him again. Alan was much stronger than he looked, but I think maybe he's crazy and I heard crazy people are really strong. He knocked Georgie off his feet. Georgie banged against the building and I heard a little ping sound, then he fell down on the concrete porch and grabbed his elbow.

"I'm cut," he said.

His face turned white.

"I warned him," Alan said.

I looked where Georgie fell against the building. There was a row of window panes on each side of the door. There was a hole in the middle of one and there was blood on the glass. I looked back at Georgie. He still had his hand over his elbow and there was blood coming out between his fingers.

"We gotta call an ambulance," I said.

I turned around to look for Dan 'cause he lived closest, but he was gone. A black lady was running across the parking lot at us. She ran up and grabbed Georgie's arm with both hands and squeezed it real tight. He started to cry.

It was Mrs. Benton, Dan's mom. I didn't recognize her when she was running at us. She explained to Georgie that she was a nurse, and that Dan was calling for an ambulance. She had to hold his arm tight like that to stop the bleeding.

"I wish I didn't have to hurt you," she said, "but it's the only way."

Georgie nodded at her. She looked at Alan.

"I warned him," Alan said.

She didn't care.

"Take off your belt," she said.

He didn't argue. He took it off and held it out to her and stood there holding up his pants with the other hand. Mrs. Benton looked at me.

"Take that belt and put it around Georgie's arm," she said, "right below my hands."

I did it. It took me awhile 'cause my hands were shaking.

"Pull it tight," she said.

I did that. Georgie whimpered some. Mrs. Benton took the belt from me and pulled it tighter. Georgie whimpered some more. Mrs. Benton looked at me again.

"Do you know where Georgie lives?" she said.

I nodded.

"Go tell his mother to come down here now. Tell her Georgie is hurt, but everything is okay because I know what to do. Okay?"

I nodded and ran away. Georgie's building was real close but it seemed to take forever to get there. I banged on his door and yelled for his mom but there was no answer. I heard that nasty cat yowling inside.

I ran back to where Georgie was hurt and told Dan's mom what happened. She nodded at me.

"I warned him," Alan said.

He was still standing in the same place, holding up his pants with the same hand.

"I'll go try again," I said.

I ran back over to Georgie's apartment and banged on the door some more and yelled again. The cat didn't yowl this time. I went back to Dan's mom and told her no luck.

"It's okay, son," she said. "They'll be here in time."

I stood around and watched her hold the belt tight on Georgie's arm. He looked the same. His face was white, but not any whiter that I could see. I took a big breath and felt my heart pounding.

"I warned him," Alan said.

I heard the ambulance coming down the road. I looked up and saw the lights flashing through the trees. It came screeching in the side entrance of the apartment complex and skidded to a stop next to F building. A young black guy and an older white guy jumped out.

"I'm a nurse," Dan's mom yelled. "This boy's a hemophiliac. I'm going to hold this belt on his arm the whole way to the hospital. Okay?"

The two men nodded. They picked the rest of Georgie up and the three of them carried him into the back of the ambulance. The young black guy ran around front and got back behind the wheel. The sirens and the lights came back on and they took off.

It was really quiet when they were gone. A bunch of people had come outside and were standing around. They started to leave.

"I warned him," Alan said.

❖ ❖ ❖

Georgie was all right. The hospital got him in plenty of time and did whatever it is they do to stop a bleeder from bleeding to death.

It turned out his mom was at my place, talking with my mom. She came over looking for Georgie and they got to talking. She liked to think that he had friends and I was one of them. I told her about his getting cut and she ran screaming out of our apartment and jumped in her car and got pulled over by a cop on the way to the hospital. She told him what was up and he put the sirens on and led her over there.

They kept Georgie overnight and his mom kept him in for three days. We thought he'd come out bragging about the hospital again, but he didn't. He didn't say much of anything. We were outside behind Alan's building and Georgie walked up and said hi.

"Hey," I said. "You all right?"

He nodded.

"I warned you," Alan said.

Georgie looked at him.

"I know," he said.

That was it. No more Georgie the Pusher. We stood around for a while, then we started playing again. We organized a game of Army. It seemed a good idea to make Georgie a sniper, since he'd just got out the hospital. A sniper shot people from a window of a building's stairwell, so it wasn't as rough as being a soldier. You didn't have to fall down and roll around when you got shot.

Georgie was pretty quiet and went along with whatever we decided. We played other stuff after Army, and he was pretty quiet about that stuff too. He was quiet all the time after that.

Alan was too, at first. He didn't say much of anything till Georgie was out of the hospital and his mom let him go outside. Then Alan was his old self, only worse. He butt in more and his comments were even weirder. Dan and I were talking about baseball one time and Alan cut in with this comment how Dan's mom had a nice ass and what he wanted to do with it. I thought Dan was going to cream him, but he just shook his head and didn't say anything. I've noticed that Dan has a lot of patience with people who aren't right.

None of us ever liked Alan, we just let him hang around 'cause we felt sorry for him. But he got too weird after the whole thing with Georgie and we started avoiding him. He caught us a couple times and we lied and said we weren't. Finally we couldn't take it anymore, and Dan told him to his face that we didn't like him and didn't want him around. Alan told us to get fucked and started crying. We stood around for a while and watched him cry, then we wandered off. He yelled at us that we were fuckers.

Georgie moved away the next summer. His mom married some guy who had a house. He never again pushed anyone, or talked about going to the hospital. He stopped telling us he was a bleeder all the time, and when new kids came around, we had to tell them 'cause he wouldn't.

Alan still lives here. All the rest of us have gotten a lot bigger, but not him. He's sixteen now and he still looks like he's twelve.

I saw him out on his back steps again last night. He was sitting under that same door light, smoking one of those little cigars. He probably swiped it from his dad. There was a magazine on the step next to him. I bet it was one of his dad's *Playboys*. His dad still gets the chicks.

His dad has a new car, a red Corvette. I watched Alan wash it the other day. He didn't know I was looking. I saw him spit on it.

Nick the Greek

On Christmas Eve of his junior year, Nick the Greek decided to commit suicide. He had his reasons. His mother had died over the summer and his father had become a haunted shuffling shell. Then a few days after Thanksgiving, Nick found his pretty little blond girlfriend in his roommate's big muscular arms.

Women, he muttered to himself.

His black mood was not improved by the bad acid he swallowed early in the evening or the flat beer he poured down after it. Nor did it help to keep such depressing company. His dorm was abandoned to the abandoned, left to those too broke to go home, those with no homes to go to, and those with no desire to see their homes.

A witty chap with John Lennon glasses pointed out these categories of familial disassociation during the dismal "party" where Nick ingested the bad acid. The witty chap put himself in the last category, and had mused quite amusingly about his family's congenital alcoholism. That is, it seemed quite humorous to Nick, who was having a good laugh, but then the witty chap punched him. Nick tried to strike back, but he found himself restrained, and as best he could recall, he was forcibly ejected from the "party."

No great loss, he concluded.

Nick wandered back to his room, trying to decide which of the witty chap's categories he belonged to. He didn't have the cash for a train ticket, but his dad would have spotted it if Nick had called ahead, so he couldn't plead poverty. Without his mother, it didn't seem that he actually had a home. And he certainly didn't want to spend any time at the musty tomb that passed for one.

Firmly on the cusp of two and three, he decided.

It was back in his room that Nick had the urge to kill himself. He never pondered his actions till after they were completed, so he climbed out the window, up the fire escape, and onto the roof. It was snowing heavily and had been for eight days. He wandered around for a while, contemplating which leap looked most fatal, but he couldn't see much in the dark and the falling snow. He eventually arrived back where he started, two stories above his room and four stories over the dormitory's parking lot.

He said a prayer: *God rest my weary soul.* Then he jumped.

Right into a big soft snowdrift. It must have been fifteen feet deep. He sat at the bottom of it, looking up out of his powdery white crater, and admired the snowflakes as they drifted down toward his upturned face. His mind cleared and his thoughts were little ones: how a particular flake sparkled as it passed by a lit window, how his nose tickled for an instant when a flake landed on it.

He sat there long enough to get pretty damn cold. He wasn't dressed for the weather and here he was buried in snow. It took him a little while to maul his way out. Then he stomped around the parking lot till most the snow fell off his clothes, banged through the dorm's metal and glass doors, climbed the worn marble steps to the third floor, and went down the hall and into his room. He undressed, dried himself off, and checked for injuries.

He didn't find any. All his parts and pieces seemed intact, as best he could tell through the bad acid, which made his arms and legs look odd and their movements appear abrupt and flailing. He put on some dry clothes, which was hard to do with his strange appendages, until he stopped thinking about it.

When he was dressed again, he stood in the middle of the room and stared at his roommate's bed, remembering what it looked like when he walked in and saw the big goon's ass bobbing up and down. And then he remembered what it felt like when he realized Annette was underneath those heavily muscled buttocks. His stomach turned and he felt lightheaded, so he sat down on his bed and stared at the floor. He sighed and rubbed his nose with the back of his hand. The feeling passed and his stomach settled down.

Nick thought about his failed jump. Maybe he needed more altitude in these snowy conditions. He remembered that the doors at the back of the dormitory led into the basement because the dorm was built on a hill. That meant that on the back side of the building, the roof was another story above ground.

Nick went to his closet, pulled out a scarf and a heavy coat and put them on, taking care to button the coat all the way up. He went back out his window, up the fire escape, and across the roof to the rear of the building. This side overlooked a sloping lawn instead of a parking lot, but pavement had failed him so he would try dirt and grass.

He said his prayer again: *God rest my weary soul.* Then he jumped again.

Right into an even deeper snowdrift. This one had to be at least twenty feet deep. He sat at the bottom of his second snow crater and laughed until a few tears ran down his flushed cheeks, and kept laughing until the tears froze.

Women, he muttered to himself.

His left ankle gave a twinge. He tried moving it: sprained. No hurry. He could rest here a bit.

❖ ❖ ❖

He sat in the snow, snug in his heavy coat, and remembered his last trip to Greece. That was two summers prior, between his freshman and sophomore years. He went with two new college buddies. *Let me show you my homeland*, he had said. *But you were born and raised in New Jersey*, they had said. *No matter*, he had said. *I am Greek.*

So they bummed around the islands, chasing girls and swilling beer. For the first week, his buddies had deferred to his Greekness and let him play tour guide. But he bullshitted them one time too many, and his limited Greek was unnecessary given the natives' superior English, so he wound up tagging along after the other two and their second-hand copy of *Let's Go Greece.* They wanted to drink less and see more, and he found himself getting out of bed much earlier than he preferred to go look at heaps of dusty rocks.

One evening on Thira, his buddies picked up a pair of Dutch girls, and they all went out to dinner. The girls were pretty, blond, and asexual, a combination that drove Nick wild. Instead of keeping quiet and letting the other four sort out who was with whom, he talked incessantly, telling every story he could think of, butchering fact and plausibility with staggering abandon.

Their waiter was a distinguished-looking small-statured man with gray hair and a knowing impassive face. When he came to deliver the check, Nick seized it, and in his unceasing expansion, attempted to engage the older man in conversation, using his gruesome Greek. The waiter grimaced slightly and switched back to English. Seeing that this had failed to bond them, Nick said:

I, too, am Greek.

The waiter watched him for a moment, with an expression of tolerance and patience that was extremely humiliating.

No, he said. *I* am Greek. *You* are Greek-American.

Nick's dining companions roared their laughter while the waiter spun on his heel and returned to the kitchen.

❖ ❖ ❖

It took Nick considerably more time and effort to maul his way out of the second snowdrift. His ankle complained whenever he used his left leg and cried bitterly when he finally stood up. The back doors into the basement were locked and sparks of pain shot up his leg while he limped around to the front of the dormitory and hobbled up the old marble stairs. Back in his room, he shed his coat and peeled off his boots and socks. His ankle was numb now and the swelling wasn't too bad. The bottoms of his jeans were snow-crusted and damp. He dug a dry pair out of his dirty laundry.

When he was dressed again, he picked up the phone to call home and punched in half the number before he noticed the line was dead. He looked at the silent receiver and realized he hadn't paid a phone bill all semester. He had to tell someone what had just happened and there wasn't anyone in this arctic hell he could talk to.

So he decided to write his brother a letter. He sat at the small wooden desk the college provided and found some paper and a pen.

> *Dear Tinos,*
> *How ya been, yadda yadda yadda. Me, I been jumpin off buildings. No joke. Did it twice cause twice is nicer. All I got was a twisted ankle. Why the fuck did mom have to die.*
> *Love, Nick*
> *P.S. Caught Annette balling Muscles.*

He read it twice, crumpled it up and threw it at the trashcan. He missed.

Women, he muttered to himself.

Nick put his paper and pen away. He stayed at the desk and examined its scarred surface. Lover's initials and curse words and the names of controlled substances and beer brands were carved into the wood. Early in the semester he had almost made the mistake of adding Annette's name to this clutter, but the tip of his cheap pocketknife had broken off. He looked for the single gouge he had made and couldn't find it.

Nick stood up, reached his bed in a single limp, and lay on his back with his hands on his stomach. Having failed at killing himself and having lost the desire to try, having no one to socialize with and no solitary interests, Nick did what he always did when the obvious possibilities exhausted themselves: he slept. Like a soft, overfed, acid-addled, semi-drunk, Greek-American baby. He had a long dream about chasing his friends around the Acropolis.

❖ ❖ ❖

"Wake the fuck up."

The voice entered Nick's dreamworld and came out the mouth of a nymph he was pursuing. The nymph looked like Annette with longer hair and shapelier legs. The voice was male so the effect was disconcerting.

"Come on, asshole. Wake up."

This time the nymph's mouth remained immobile. She shrugged and disappeared. Nick recognized the voice as belonging to his brother Tinos. *How did Tinos get to Ancient Greece?* was Nick's next thought. Then he felt a vibration on his right side. Tinos was shaking Nick's arm.

"Wake up, wake up. Wake the fuck up."

Nick was stiff all over, his mouth was dry and crusted, and his head felt compressed. He was still lying on his back. He cracked one eye and pointed it at his brother.

"What're you doin' here."

"Gettin' you, asshole."

Nick opened his other eye. He blinked a few times.

"Why?"

Tinos shrugged.

"Dad's mopin' around the house like Mom died all over again. He said he misses you."

He kicked the side of Nick's mattress.

"Come on, get up."

The jarring motion made Nick's stomach roll. He sat up and put his feet on the floor. Tinos kicked the bed again.

"Get the fuck up and let's get some breakfast. I'm starvin'. I've been driving all fuckin' night."

"Allright, allright."

Nick stumbled to his feet and gimped around the room. He left the clothes on that he had fallen asleep in, put his boots back on without tying the laces, stuffed his laundry into a duffel bag, and limped down to his brother's truck.

They were in a diner near the highway before they spoke again.

"What's wrong with yer ankle."

"Sprained it."

"How."

Nick watched his brother devour eggs and potatoes. A piece of toast went down in three bites.

"I jumped off my dorm last night."

Tinos snorted into his plate. He didn't even bother to look up.

"You are *sooo* full of shit," was all Tinos said.

Typical replies came to Nick's mind: *No I'm not! I'm serious, man! Fuck you!* He didn't say any of them. He didn't say anything. For the first time in his life, he considered the merits of the charge. And Nick the Greek did not argue.

Reefer Diamond

1

Diamond Hazelette was 300 pounds in her bra and panties, which was all she happened to be wearing when the SWAT team surrounded her trailer. She was an observant woman, some would say paranoid, and when she looked out her bathroom window and glimpsed a patch of dark blue moving through the scrub pines, she went and got her rifle.

She had dated a cop once, many years back, when she only weighed about 200 pounds. His name was Chester James and she wondered if he was out there in the pine trees and poison oak while she slipped shells into her 30/30. Their relationship had ended badly, when Chester gave her cousin Princess a speeding ticket. The way Diamond saw it, what good was screwing a cop if it didn't protect your kin from a goddamn ticket?

She went back to the bathroom, looked back out the window. Nothing moved, blue or otherwise. She sat sideways on the toilet and waited.

Her affair with Chester had ended in the dirt drive out front. She told him her thoughts on sex, law officers, kin, and speeding tickets. He said that Princess had offered him sexual favors to rescind the ticket. Diamond pointed toward the highway, and Chester left. They never exchanged another word and her affection for Princess never wavered. Diamond didn't really blame Princess if she did offer herself. Chester was a good-looking man, and Princess was poor as dirt.

Movement caught her eye—a blue shoulder between some pine branches. She aimed three feet above where she guessed the officer's head would be and squeezed the trigger. The roar was deafening in the little bathroom, but she had expected that. She was out in the living room, crouched next to the open front door, before the echo faded down the holler.

Halfway up the ridge behind her trailer, on a rounded shoulder that got an abundance of sun, surrounded by thorny locust trees, brambly blackberries, and a ring of barbed wire, was a patch of fifty female marijuana plants. The males were carefully culled so that they wouldn't pollinate the females and turn their blossoms to seed; seedless female blossoms yield by far the greatest potency. None of the plants were less than eight feet tall and it was still early in the season.

Diamond knew that just one of those plants could cost her five years in prison. She assumed that meant the patch could put her away for well past the end of her natural life. She would rather be shot dead in her trailer.

After a few moments of crouching next to her front door, it occurred to Diamond that if the cops had simply worn camouflage, as any idiot looking to hide in the woods would do, she would be in custody by now.

"Stupid goddamn cops," she mumbled.

She shook her big head, then looked down at her undressed self. Her enormous bosom stretched her worn-out brassiere and a new pair of vast pink panties rode up her ass.

"Damn fool position to be in," she muttered. "Prac'ly nekkid."

She pictured herself in handcuffs and her undergarments, being marched through a crowd into the Bevel Springs Police Station, flashbulbs popping like an old movie. The image made her mad. She shook her big head again.

Diamond was crouched down next to the open door, below the glass in the top half of the storm door. She never bothered to put in a screen so it was a storm door year round. She heard movement out front, so she raised herself just enough to peek outside.

She didn't see anything, no telltale patch of blue. She watched and waited. She thought she heard more motion, off to her right, but couldn't be sure. She watched and waited a little more—then something told Diamond there had been a change in her favor, that a window of opportunity had opened, that it was time to move. And when her animal instincts said go, Diamond Hazelette went.

Still crouching, she slowly turned the handle on the storm door. When it was unlatched, she bunched her legs up beneath her, then gave a mighty lunge out into the daylight. Holding the rifle down at her waist, she fired one quick shot straight ahead, at nothing in particular, then cut sharply to her left, into the nearest patch of trees.

When a cop popped up in her way, she knocked him over with a straight arm and ran right over him. She never looked back.

2

The cops didn't know about the pot plants. Most of them wouldn't have cared. Marijuana was the moonshine of their era: too many people they knew, or were related to, were smoking it and growing it for them to take it seriously as a law enforcement issue.

They were looking for Willis Hazelette, Diamond's nephew, who was wanted for a bank robbery committed the previous day. A tip placed him in the vicinity of Diamond's trailer late that morning. Since there wasn't much else up her way, here they were.

The first shot was unexpected. The dirt drive was empty—Diamond's car was in the shop—and the trailer was silent, so they assumed no one was home.

"Anyone hit?"

It was the officer in command, Lieutenant Roy Burkhead, addressing his men over their walkie-talkie headsets. He was in his early fifties, about six one, lean and rope-muscled, with steel gray hair and eyes. He was, at this moment, completely in his element.

"Weber, sir. Not hit, but injured anyway."

"How?" Burkhead snapped.

Glenn Weber was a stocky ex-high school football player, gone thoroughly to fat in his thirtieth year. His was the blue shoulder Diamond had spotted. Weber grimaced at his commanding officer's tone and at knowing the entire SWAT team was listening to this conversation. When he shifted his weight some in nervousness, pain from his ankle shot up his leg.

"Shit," he hissed.

"Excuse me?" Burkhead hissed back.

"Sorry sir. My ankle's busted."

"What happened?"

Weber paused, sighed, then owned up to it.

"I ducked and slipped on some rocks."

Some muffled snickering came over the headsets.

"No humor in this that I can see," Burkhead said.

The snickering stopped.

"Anyone see anything?" he asked.

No reply.

"Weber, I'm coming around for you. Everyone else, lay low."

Burkhead moved further away from the trailer, back into the underbrush. In his exasperation with the downed Weber, he was a little less careful than usual, and made more noise than he normally would. The sounds he made went into the trailer and reached the attentive ears of Diamond Hazelette. While Diamond peeked out the storm door window, Burkhead slipped quickly and almost silently around to the back of the trailer.

He did not expect Weber's ankle to be broken. He knew that a bad sprain could hurt enough to convince its victim that a bone had snapped. But Weber's bulk had come down on his ankle exactly wrong, leaving it at an angle only a break could allow. He wouldn't be limping out of there.

"Shit," Burkhead said.

The other men listened intently to the faint static hiss in their headsets.

"Officer James, sir. Is everything all right?"

Lieutenant Burkhead glared at Glen Weber, then turned his attention back to the ankle.

"The ankle's fucked. We'll have to carry him out."

He was considering how to reassign his men when Diamond Hazelette fired her second shot and burst from the trailer.

"Report!" Burkhead barked.

The retort from Diamond's gun was still echoing down the holler.

"Sweet Jesus, what was that?" an officer said.

There was a thumping noise in the headsets.

"Report!" Burkhead barked again.

No reply, just some muffled laughing.

"What the fuck's going on!" Burkhead bellowed.

The echo of the shot finally died. A moment or two passed, then there was a clattering sound in the headsets.

"Officer James, sir."

His voice was tight and cramped-sounding.

"We seem to have disturbed the lady of the house."

Lieutenant Burkhead tried to ask Chester James what he meant, but no one could hear him over the laughter. He waited two seconds, then took off the headset and yelled:

"Shut the fuck up!"

He was unbelievably loud. The laughing ended immediately. He put his headset back on.

"James, report."

"Well sir, Diamond Hazelette came chargin' outta her house an' ran me over."

"Who fired?"

"She did."

"Where is she?"

"She took off up the mountain."

"Well follow her, asshole!"

Burkhead left Glen Weber where he lay and took off after Chester James. He yelled names and orders into his headset, and pretty soon four men were on their way up the ridge and three men were securing the trailer. Glen Weber sat by himself and silently wished he had followed his father into the extermination trade.

❖ ❖ ❖

Chester James did not exert his best effort in the pursuit of Diamond Hazelette. She had left him flat on his back, with his wind knocked out, so he didn't see where she went—not that he wanted to catch her.

When Chester and Diamond stood out in her dirt drive and discussed sex, law officers, kin, and speeding tickets, Chester told a big fat lie. The truth was that Chester had solicited sexual favors from Princess in exchange for rescinding the ticket, and Princess had refused. He suspected Diamond and Princess would have discussed the matter, and Diamond was sure to believe Princess when she denied Chester's accusation, since Princess was known for her honesty and Chester was a born liar. Chester's only doubt came from Diamond's inaction in the meantime: it would be more in keeping with her character to have confronted Chester immediately following the revelations from Princess.

Chester saw today's events playing out in two possible ways. First, Diamond might shoot him, and she was a good shot. Second, he could imagine a scene between himself, Diamond, and Lieutenant Roy Burkhead, with the rest of the SWAT team as witnesses, in which Diamond related the proposal Chester James had made to Princess. Burkhead was a notorious tight-ass, and Chester was certain there was no way he could slip that noose unhung. Since his break-up with Diamond over Princess's ticket, Officer Chester James had racked up two similar complaints from the female citizenry. He was on probation as a result.

So he wasn't running when Lieutenant Burkhead came up next to him. He wasn't even walking. He was just standing in a small clearing, hands on hips, staring off into space.

"Don't tell me you didn't see where she went," Burkhead said.

"I'm sorry, sir."

"Oh goddamn."

While the Lieutenant studied the ground, the other two officers he had assigned to the chase finally caught up. Burkhead found Diamond's trail, about forty feet to the right, and off they all went.

Officer James brought up the rear. His thoughts alternated between the task at hand and his past sins. He made a sincere prayer that he might find the strength to absolve himself of his misconduct. He was starting to feel a little better when the officer ahead of him yelled:

"Sweet Jesus and Mary, will you look at that!"

They had crossed the barbed wire and burst through the briar thickets and come into clear view of Diamond's marijuana crop. Even Roy Burkhead was temporarily distracted, like a bloodhound that accidentally comes across a nice piece of steak.

"Well, boys, I guess we know why she ran," he said.

Which immediately reminded him that they were still on the hunt. He left Officer James to guard the weed lest Diamond return, and he took off up the ridge with the other two men in tow.

It was rough going. The first obstacle was the dense thicket they tracked her into. The second problem was Diamond's slippery trail. Before they had followed the faint path to her pot patch, but now they were tracking her over unbroken ground. She proved quite elusive for a woman the size of a small bear.

They hit their third obstacle when they cleared the thicket. They found themselves climbing off the gentle shoulder that cradled Diamond's herb garden and going straight up the side of the main ridge. They had to grab trees as they went to keep from tumbling backward. Burkhead was astounded that a woman as big and round as Diamond Hazelette could make it up such a slope.

"What's she made of, crazy glue?" he suddenly barked.

The other officers didn't make out what he said. They were too busy gasping for breath. When they found Burkhead waiting at the bottom of a rock cliff, they collapsed at his feet and panted like dogs. Burkhead pointed at the rocks above and said:

"No way that fat bitch made it over this."

Then he stood around with a pissed off expression on his face. He looked up again, then looked one way along the bottom of the cliff, then the other. He cursed some, but not very loudly. When his two followers had stopped gasping like beached fish, he sent them south along the bottom of the cliff, and went north himself.

3

Willis Hazelette was nowhere near his aunt's trailer on the morning the SWAT team surrounded it. After he robbed a branch of the Blue Ridge Bank the day before, he promptly skipped the state. He had friends in a nasty little law-hating inbred redneck town way up in a dank West Virginia holler. A little graft to the right folks and he was as safe up there as he would be in Brazil.

He was drinking in the only bar for thirty miles, a low-roofed falling-down shack with an expired liquor license. Willis had already bought the half-empty house two rounds. He was cocky and loud, happily swapping outrageous lies with the short tattoed man sitting next to him, the fellow lowlife who had served as his getaway driver.

Over the bar, the evening news came on the television. No one paid any attention until a newscaster mentioned Willis's name, then a church-like hush descended. The bartender glided over to the set and gently turned up the volume. Willis smiled like a baby while the newscasters and two field reporters breathlessly related the details of his crime and the ongoing manhunt. He savored every detail, and the bar crowd seemed to bask in his reflected glory.

When Diamond's picture suddenly appeared next to the male newscaster's head, Willis grinned in friendly recognition.

"How do, Auntie," he yelled.

Nervous laughter went around the room. The photograph was an older shot, taken when Diamond got a short-lived job at Wal-Mart. She probably only weighed about 250 or so. Then the anchor started her story.

"They're calling her Reefer Diamond, the marijuana queen of central Virginia."

Willis's face collapsed into a worried frown and his fans made a murmur of anxiety. The newscaster smirked while he described the events at Diamond's trailer, and practically leered when he stated what she was wearing when last seen. He smirked some more when he mentioned that she had knocked over an officer when she burst from her trailer.

"And as fate would have it," he intoned, "*that* officer—"

He made a big show of looking at the other anchor, who was off-camera.

"—you're not gonna believe this, Jen—"

He turned back to the camera.

"—but that officer was a *former boyfriend.*"

The screen cut to a wide shot of the two anchors laughing and shaking their heads.

"That's just *too much*," the vaguely Asian-looking female anchor said.

"Tell me about it!" the male anchor replied.

He was a black-haired chisel-chinned back-slapper who had started out covering sports. He went on with the story about Diamond, and when the screen showed footage of DEA agents chopping down Diamond's patch, Willis almost fell off his stool.

"Goddamn, Auntie!" he bellowed.

The male anchor wrapped up the story with another smirk while he said that Diamond was still "at large," all but winking when he said those two words, then frowned intently while relating that she was considered armed and dangerous. Despite his attempt at seriousness, it was somehow apparent that he didn't see how a fat lady like Diamond could be any sort of trouble.

Willis Hazelette, carefree despite being the subject of an FBI manhunt, now had something to worry about.

"Aw, damn," he said. "Aunt Diamond's gonna kill me."

The room fell silent. The bartender glided back over to the set and eased the volume back down. He drifted over to Willis and caressingly served him a fresh beer. Willis looked up into the older man's face, which was a mess of lines and small scars.

"That's just how she is, you see. She's gonna be hoppin' mad 'bout all this, an' someone's gotta be blamed. It's gonna be me, I jus' know it. Hell, this is a damn lousy break."

He chewed his fingernails for a bit.

"She was talkin' 'bout buildin' a house. She hates livin' in a trailer. Wanted a real roof over her head. I asked her where she was gonna get the money, she just laughed at me, said it wasn' my business."

He looked up at the television.

"Guess I went and made it my business."

The bartender waited till Willis's last words had faded, till the young felon's face had softened slightly.

"But Willis, watcha so worried about? No one knows yer here. How she gonna find you?"

Willis glanced at the old man, with both sheepishness and resentment, then snorted lightly. He turned his attention back to the television set.

"Who d'ya think told me 'bout this place?" he finally said.

4

She hadn't meant to run to her pot patch, but when she took off up the ridge, her feet went the way they knew best. The last of it, through the thorns and briars and over the barbed wire, wasn't easy half-naked. She was scraped and scratched all over. But that wasn't the worst of it. Once she got there, she realized it could be a dead end. She had always gone in and out but one way, and the far side of the plot was particularly dense and brambled.

"Goddamn my fuckin' luck," Diamond muttered.

She gave herself a moment to think. She didn't hear anyone behind her yet, and her hearing had always been acute. She looked longingly at her marijuana plants. They were going to be her ticket out of that trailer, the down payment on that little two-bedroom house she was going to build herself. The way the crop had turned out, it could have financed the entire construction.

She put down her rifle and stepped out of her panties. She used the pink cotton underwear to wrap up a bundle of buds from the nearest plant. They were as green as cash and almost as liquid. She stuffed the package into her cleavage, picked up her rifle, jumped the barbed wire with considerable grace, and disappeared into the thicket towards the top of the mountain. The thorns worked hard on her, but she kept her mouth shut, and slipped through surprisingly fast.

It took Diamond about two hours to scramble over the ridge and make her way down the valley on the other side. She passed a hunter along the way—a poacher actually, considering that nothing was in season—but he didn't notice the 300-pound near-naked woman who watched him from behind a pile of rocks. She glanced down at her buff-colored legs and white pelvis and thought, *damned fool catch a glimpse a me, he'd think I's a white-tail deer.*

Diamond had a friend who lived in this valley, a black woman named Lula Granger. She wasn't as big as Diamond, but she was big enough that Diamond hoped she might be able to squeeze into some of Lula's clothes. Lula's door was open and the screen door wasn't latched. Diamond knocked for a little while, then went inside.

"Lula?" she called.

There was no answer. Diamond left her rifle next to the front door and checked the other rooms. That didn't take long because there weren't many of them. Lula wasn't home. Her truck was in the drive, so she was probably out on foot. She made extra money gathering roots and herbs.

Diamond went to the kitchen and found a baggie for her dope. She took the bundle from her cleavage and unwrapped it. The heady aroma of fresh-picked marijuana filled the room. Diamond put her panties back on, then said:

"That'll make m' privates smell nice."

She put the rewrapped pot back in her cleavage and went to Lula's bedroom. She found some blue jeans and a tee shirt that looked appropriate for avoiding the law. She tried them on.

"Goddamn, Lula, yer gettin' as fat as me."

The pants hung about two inches above her ankles, but otherwise the fit was tolerable. She had less luck with shoes; Lula's feet were too small. Diamond had almost resigned herself to staying barefoot when she came across a nice pair of men's work boots that weren't too huge. Lula had never married and the boots looked fairly new. Diamond wondered who Lula was keeping company with.

There were a few dollars in an old coffee can on the dresser. Diamond stuffed them into a pocket. She came across the keys to the truck when she picked up a soap opera magazine. This was the hard part—she had no problem making off with clothes and small money, but stealing Lula's wheels seemed pretty low indeed. The truck wasn't worth more then four or five hundred bucks, but that was a lot of money to a woman like Lula, and taking it would leave her stranded.

Diamond snatched up the keys and went back to the kitchen. She gulped some water from the sink, pilfered some food for the road, and retrieved her rifle on her way out the front door. She went out into the drive and climbed into the old pickup. She turned the key and the engine churned and shrugged into action. Diamond stepped on the gas and started down the old rutted holler road. She bumped along for the three miles it took to reach blacktop. Then she sat at the stop sign and looked up and down the two-lane country highway.

She turned south and eased the truck up to fifty. It didn't rattle as much as she expected. After a mile or so, she turned on the radio. A lady country singer moaned plaintively about a love that wasn't true, and then the news announcer came on. He talked about the stock market and the Middle East and some other crap that Diamond didn't care about. She took her foot off the gas when she heard him say:

"Next, they're calling her Reefer Diamond, the marijuana queen of central Virginia. Stay tuned, and we'll tell you more."

Her foot was still in the air, hovering over the pedals, and she was slowly drifting to a stop. A little sedan came up close behind her, braked hard, then jumped on the gas and zipped past. Diamond flinched as it went by, then pulled over on the side of the road, put the truck in park, and waited for the commercials to end.

When the news came back on, she sat frozen through most of the story, her head canted toward the big speaker in the dash. They covered it completely, starting with the manhunt for Willis and climaxing with Diamond's coronation as "the marijuana queen." She only reacted once, chuckling quietly when they related how she had run over her former boyfriend. In all the excitement, she hadn't recognized Chester James. He was just a man in blue in her way.

When the story was over, she sat still for another minute or two, through the rest of the news and into the sports. Her face was alternately dark and ecstatic.

"Willis, you stupid bastard," she finally said.

Diamond put the truck back in gear and swung out onto the asphalt. She plucked Lula's sunglasses from the visor and tried them on. She looked at herself in the big outside mirror and smiled with wry satisfaction.

At the next crossroad, she turned west. She jacked up the volume on the country music station and sang along the whole way to the state line. As she passed the beat up old sign that said, "Welcome to West Virginia," she bellowed at the top of her lungs:

"Watch out, Willis, you stupid bastard. Reefer Diamond's comin' t' getcha."

She was still laughing a mile down the road.

La Estupidez de Cosas

Rush hour was over but traffic in the city was still bad. The long summer days kept the streets busy. Chuy did not like this drive and did not enjoy going to his sister's. His mood got worse by the mile.

His sister lived on the south side, in a neighborhood of little off-white stucco houses with black iron bars on the windows and doors. It wasn't the worst neighborhood in the city, wasn't even considered one of the bad ones. But it was bad enough to Chuy. He didn't understand why his sister left Los Huertos. Now property in the village was so expensive she couldn't afford to move back.

The streets were empty in his sister's neighborhood. Chuy guessed everyone was still inside eating dinner, or slumped in front of their TV sets. He could hear TVs blaring from some of the houses. It was quiet otherwise, quiet except for the constant hum of the highway. You could see Route 40 from the patch of gravel that was his sister's front yard.

As Chuy turned into his sister's little dead-end street, his nephew Tomas came out the front door of their little house. Tomas was small and fine-boned. He would enter eleventh grade in the fall. They waved to each other and Tomas met Chuy's truck at the curb.

"How's it hangin', Unc?"

Chuy shook his head.

"I hate the damn traffic."

Tomas nodded.

"Yeah. Me too. Thanks for comin' down."

Chuy shrugged.

"Sure."

He climbed out of his truck and followed Tomas to an old Malibu parked in the short driveway. It had been bleached by the desert sun to a flat gray-blue.

"Payne's gray," Chuy said.

"Huh?"

Chuy gestured at the car with his chin.

"I was looking at paint chips today. They called this color Payne's gray."

Tomas looked at his car.

"Huh," he said.

Chuy poked his chin at the car again.

"Tell me again what's wrong."

Tomas described the trouble he was having. A rough idle they thought they'd fixed was back. The car choked going into second gear. He popped the hood and they stared at the engine. It was gray too, a dull greasy gray.

Pain's gray, Chuy thought, and laughed quietly.

"What's funny, Unc?"

Chuy considered explaining this pun to his nephew.

"Nothing," he said. "Where's your tools?"

❖ ❖ ❖

A half hour later Chuy had the idle back under control. He and Tomas were gathered around the engine again, listening to it hum. Tomas stood at the front of the fender on the driver's side and Chuy stood across from him. Chuy wiped his hands on a rag and tossed it backhand over the engine to Tomas. The boy caught the rag and wiped his hands too.

"Hey Unc," Tomas said. "I almost forgot."

Chuy looked at his nephew. Tomas tilted his head toward Chuy's truck.

"You know the gangbanger stole your wheels?"

Chuy nodded. Tomas straightened his head. He held the rag by a corner and spun it around in circles. Chuy frowned.

"He's dead," Tomas said.

Chuy's stomach tightened. The backs of his hands went cool.

"What?"

Tomas nodded. He stopped spinning the rag, then started again.

"What happened?" Chuy said.

"They stabbed 'im."

"Where?"

Tomas shrugged.

"Somewhere that killed him."

Chuy leaned over and put his hands on the top of the fender. He looked down at the idling engine.

"I meant where was he. I thought he was still in prison."

"He was."

Chuy looked up at Tomas.

"Who stabbed him?"

Tomas stopped spinning the rag.

"Someone from his gang. They say he was cuttin' a deal with the cops."

Chuy squinted at his nephew, then looked back down at the engine.

"How do you know about it?"

Tomas shrugged.

"His aunt or something lives near here. It's all over the neighborhood."

Chuy nodded once. He watched the engine vibrate. He took a deep breath and tapped an index finger against sheet metal.

"Shut it off," he said.

His voice was hard. Tomas froze for a second, then slipped his head and shoulders inside the driver's window and cut the ignition. When he was standing next to the open hood again, Chuy looked him in the eye.

"Tell me you're not in his gang."

"I'm not in *any* gang."

Chuy stared at him for a long moment.

"You're telling me the truth."

Tomas nodded.

"Say it."

"Yes. I'm telling the truth, Uncle."

Chuy stood up straight. He moved around the front of the car and stood next to Tomas. The boy turned toward Chuy and blinked up at him.

"You swear to me?" Chuy said

"I swear."

Tomas turned back toward the car.

"They don't want me."

Chuy folded his arms. He studied the side of the boy's face.

"What do you mean?"

Tomas shrugged and said nothing.

"Out with it, Tomas. What do you mean by that?"

"Like I said. They don't want me."

"And that's a bad thing?"

Tomas hesitated, then shook his head.

"Do they give you any trouble?" Chuy said.

Tomas shook his head again.

"No."

He glanced up at his uncle, then looked away.

"I'm nothing to them," he said.

Chuy watched the boy's suffering.

"And that's a bad thing?" he said again.

His voice was gentle and quiet. Tomas spread his fingers out on a fender and stared at them.

"I'm nothing to anyone," he said.

He almost whispered it. Chuy's heart lurched in his chest and he felt sick. He moved forward and wrapped an arm around his nephew's delicate shoulders.

"You're something to *me*, Tomas. You're very important to me."

Tomas still stared at his fingers. Chuy looked down at the side of the boy's face. Tomas blinked, then blinked again.

"The kid who stole my truck. They wanted him, right?"

Tomas nodded.

"And he's dead. Right?"

Tomas nodded again. Chuy squeezed him hard.

"You stay alive, Tomas. I would miss you too much."

Tomas nodded a third time. He ran the back of a greasy hand across his nose. After a moment, Chuy gestured at the engine.

"Let's get this wreck of yours out on the road and see if it still chokes going into second."

❖ ❖ ❖

They tooled around the south side for about ten minutes, going up and down through the gears. The car ran fine. Chuy was struck again by what a good driver Tomas was, confident but cautious, so unlike the typical teenage boy. They didn't talk much because Chuy was intent on the sound of the engine and Tomas knew to keep quiet. When Chuy was satisfied with his repairs, he told Tomas to head home, and that set Chuy to an old line of thought.

"How's your mother doing?" he said.

Tomas shrugged.

"Better, I guess."

"She still drinks?"

"Yeah. But not as much. She doesn't get drunk so often."

Chuy glanced at a billboard. A group of half-naked Latinas played in a fountain next to a giant beer bottle.

"You hear from your father lately?" Chuy said.

Tomas shook his head. Chuy left him alone. A few minutes later, as they turned into the little dead-end street, the front door of Tomas's house opened, and his mother stepped outside.

"Speak of the devil," Tomas said.

Chuy snorted and suppressed a grin. His sister met them in the driveway. She was still in her work clothes, the pale green uniform she wore to clean rooms at the hotel up on the highway. Her hair needed washing. She had let it down and it spilled across her shoulders and her back.

Chuy and Tomas climbed out of the car. Chuy's sister took a pack of Newports and a butane lighter from a big pocket on the front of her dress.

"How's it runnin'?" she said.

Tomas looked at Chuy.

"Good," Chuy said. "How're you?"

She shrugged and tapped a cigarette from the pack. She put it between her lips, lit it, tilted her head back, and blew smoke up in the air. She dropped the pack and the lighter back in her big pocket.

"Fine," she said.

Chuy nodded.

"Good."

Tomas fidgeted with his keys. Chuy took a deep breath. His sister let out another jet of smoke.

"I should go," Chuy said.

His sister squinted up at him.

"Sure," she said.

Chuy turned to Tomas.

"Let me know if it acts up again."

"Thanks, Unc."

"Sure."

Chuy went down the short drive and got in his truck. He started it up and pulled away. He turned around in the tight cul-de-sac at the end of the little dead-end street. His sister and his nephew were still out front when he went past. He waved at them and they waved back. His sister spoke to Tomas as Chuy turned out of the little dead-end street. Her voice bounced off the houses and the asphalt and into Chuy's truck as he accelerated away, back toward the highway and Los Huertos.

"I hate it when you call him 'Unc'," she said.

❖ ❖ ❖

The traffic on Route 40 was still bad. Chuy found himself stuck tight between two semis. He shook his head and checked his mirrors. A solid line of cars and trucks filled the passing lane as far back as he could see. He shook his head again and turned the radio on. He punched up a couple stations then snapped the radio off. He checked his mirrors a few more times, then gave up and got off at the next exit. It wasn't his usual turn; he would have to wind his way through some back streets to catch Kurtz Boulevard going north to Los Huertos.

This part of the city was tire dealers and car parts and auto repair shops. The sidewalks were always empty. There was no reason to come here that didn't involve driving. Chuy sat at a light and watched an older black man and a young Anglo lock up a body shop. The black man went south in a powder blue vintage Mustang convertible and the Anglo followed in a red Nissan Sentra with racing stripes and custom hubs and tinted windows. The Sentra turned right at the end of the block and disappeared behind a low cinderblock tire dealership.

The light changed and Chuy continued west. After a few blocks, the auto parts and supply stores were replaced by warehouses and truck terminals. The buildings were big and dark and the streets were empty. He looked down one of the wide avenues that ran north and south and saw a string of hookers posing and promenading on a dirty sidewalk. There was a cluster of them around a red Nissan Sentra with racing stripes and tinted windows. Chuy smirked and shook his head. One of the hookers got in the car.

Chuy wondered if his sister had ever sold herself. The thought came up out of nowhere and hit so hard he jerked backwards in his seat. He remembered how she looked in her ugly green uniform, her dirty hair spilling down, her cigarette with red lipstick ringing the filter so it looked like it was dipped in blood. She had a lazy insolence like the painted women on the wide avenue. He shook his head and took a deep breath. She had never been a beauty, but what she had, many men wanted—just like the street walkers. He shook his head again. He drove through empty blocks of sooty buildings. Trash blew around in the evening wind.

At the edge of the warehouse district there was a long block where street dealers fed the commuter trade. Chuy sat a stop sign and watched a transaction go down across the avenue. An Anglo businessman in a gold Lexus was buying from a kid who looked like a harder version of Tomas. Money and drugs changed hands and the Lexus took off down the block. Chuy started across the avenue and the kid gave him an expectant look. Chuy snorted and shook his head and rolled on past.

❖ ❖ ❖

Traffic was light going north on Kurtz Boulevard. The southbound lanes were busier. Chuy guessed these oncoming cars were stragglers from the day shift at Persicon. Maybe they went out for dinner in

Rancho Grande, or did some shopping before going home. Chuy wondered at a life spent making computer chips all day, in that big blocky monstrosity of a plant that looked ready to tumble off the mesa and crush Los Huertos. He could not imagine it was a good life; the smells that blew from that plant sometimes were all he needed to know. The cars kept coming and Chuy wondered when all these people would leave. He was certain they would not stay forever. This was another western boom, cast in silicon this time instead of gold or silver, and like all the others it would end.

Chuy sat at the traffic light at the end of the Boulevard and looked east to the Jitomate Mountains. They blushed the ripe tomato red that gave them their name. He looked to the west and saw pink and orange clouds piled along the bottom of the sky. Up above was pale blue. It was calm and cool here on the edge of Los Huertos. He could feel the sweet pull of the Rio Huérfano, coursing through its channel a half mile to the east.

The light changed and Chuy crossed Bosquecillo Boulevard and entered Los Huertos. He turned left at Rico's and smiled at the full parking lot; his friend Rico Lupe would be busy tonight. He turned right at the mission church, onto Entrada Oeste, then made the first left onto the narrow dirt lane that led to his house.

He looked ahead down the lane and saw a cop car back out of a driveway. He couldn't be sure at this distance but it looked to be Chuy's house. His heart fluttered a little and his stomach felt hollow. The police cruiser and Chuy's truck slowly approached each other, rumbling over the rutted dirt, dust clouds trailing out behind them. There was no breeze just now and the dust hung in the air.

The patrol car was in shadow at first, cast by a row of trees along the lane. When the car came out into the sunlight, Chuy could see that there was only the driver inside. That made him feel better; Chuy knew that bad news came with two cops. As they drew nearer, Chuy saw that the cop was an Anglo wearing sunglasses. When the Anglo pulled off his sunglasses, Chuy thought he looked familiar. Then the car was slowing down, and Chuy slowed too. The cop waved out his open window, and they drew to a stop next to each other in another patch of shade from another row of trees.

"Good evening, Mr. Sandoval."

It was the young Anglo police detective that had brought Chuy home after his truck was stolen. But now he was in uniform and driving a marked car.

"Hey," Chuy said. "I didn't recognize you."

"I'm not surprised."

"Why the change?"

The cop frowned.

"Well you see—"

Chuy grinned at him.

"You got demoted?"

The cop blushed. Chuy felt bad and stopped grinning. The cop looked straight ahead for a moment, then turned back toward Chuy.

"I'm in training. The day we met was my first day out of uniform. Most the time they still make me wear blues."

Chuy nodded.

"Okay," he said. "No big deal."

The cop shrugged, then he grinned at Chuy.

"You gonna stop making fun of me so I can tell you why I'm here?"

Chuy laughed a little, then he was serious.

"I think I know why you're here."

"Okay."

"The kid who stole my truck got killed."

The cop nodded.

"News travels fast," the cop said.

"I heard his gang killed him."

The cop hesitated, then nodded again.

"Yeah. They did."

Chuy shook his head, then frowned at the cop.

"Why'd you come to tell me?"

The cop glanced down at the dust and dirt, then looked back up at Chuy.

"I thought you'd want to know."

Chuy nodded.

"You're right. Thanks."

The cop just shrugged.

"So was the kid cutting a deal?" Chuy said.

"Is that what you heard?"

Chuy nodded. The cop nodded back.

"He screwed up before and his gang wasn't happy when he screwed up again. He cost them both times. He got scared, he turned to us, and he told the wrong person."

The cop glanced away again.

"He was a stupid kid and it caught up with him," the cop said.

Chuy watched the cop for a moment, then looked down the lane toward his house. A roadrunner popped out of the brush and onto the dirt, flicked its wings and scampered away. Chuy turned back toward the cop. The cop was looking up at the sky.

"You think the monsoons are over?" the cop said.

"Might be."

"I hope not."

"Yeah. Me too."

The cop blinked up at the blue, then looked at Chuy.

"Tell me something," Chuy said. "What made you want to become a cop?"

The Anglo smiled with half his mouth.

"I wonder that myself. My old man was a cop, his old man was a cop. My mother's old man was a cop."

Chuy nodded.

"You got any brothers?"

The Anglo nodded back.

"Three."

"Any of them cops?"

The Anglo shook his head.

"One's a fireman, one's in the air force, and the black sheep sells insurance."

Chuy snorted when he laughed.

"Two sisters," the Anglo said. "One's a nurse and the other's a schoolteacher."

"Yeah, that one brother really doesn't fit."

The Anglo smiled and shook his head.

"What about you, Mr. Sandoval? Do you have any brothers?"

Chuy shook his head.

"Not anymore. My older brother died in Vietnam and my younger one was in a car wreck."

"I'm sorry to hear that."

"Thanks. It was a long time ago."

Chuy stuck out his hand and used his thumb to point behind him and off to his left, across the hood of the police cruiser, across Los Huertos and the Rio

Huérfano, all the way across the sprawling city to their southeast.

"I have a sister down on the south side."

He let his hand fall down against his truck door.

"My nephew told me about the kid who stole my truck. The kid has family down there."

The policeman nodded. Chuy nodded back. The conversation had come full circle. The policeman put his sunglasses back on.

"Well, Mr. Sandoval, it was good talking to you."

Chuy nodded once.

"You too," he said. "Thanks again for coming by."

The policeman dipped his chin once and started off up the lane. He gave a little wave out his side window and Chuy waved back. Chuy got his truck going again. He checked the cop's progress in his mirrors. A breeze came up and blew away the dust hanging between them. When Chuy started into his drive, the police cruiser was turning left onto Entrada Oeste. Chuy expected the cop to turn right, back toward the city. For an instant he wondered what drew the policeman deeper into Los Huertos.

❖ ❖ ❖

Chuy parked his truck at the head of the drive. Teresa's station wagon wasn't there and its absence made him lonely. He got out of his truck and stood in the yard for a moment, looking up at the sky. Then he went around the house to the garden out back. He got down on one knee and began pulling weeds from between his peppers. His knees ached and that irritated him. He did not miss being young but he missed having a young man's body.

Chuy thought about his sister down in the city. He pictured her slouched before the TV set, chain-smoking Newports, dirty dishes piled in the sink and the air clogged with smoke and grease. He knew where Tomas would be, out in his car now that it was running smooth again, driving around with one of his friends, gentle awkward boys even more beaten-down than Tomas.

Chuy thought about the boy who had stolen his truck, the boy who had just died in prison. He was only a few years older than Tomas. He was slightly built, like Tomas. And now he was dead. Chuy wondered how it happened, if the boy ever knew he was about to die. He wondered if anyone truly grieved for the boy, or if the boy was as alone in this world as his death implied.

Then Chuy remembered when he caught the boy, how angry he was to see this punk driving his truck, how he pulled the boy from the cab, threw him down on the pavement, and stepped on his throat. Without Chuy, the boy would not have been in prison, and he would not be dead. Heat welled up in Chuy's belly. He resented his part in the boy's death. He felt used by fate. His motions became abrupt. He stabbed his hand at the weeds and yanked them violently from the soil.

Finally he stabbed too far and the end of his index finger smashed into a half-buried stone. Blood oozed out from under his cracked nail.

"¡La estupidez de cosas!" Chuy yelled.

It was something his grandmother used to say: "the stupidity of things." He hadn't heard the phrase since his grandmother passed away. He was surprised her words were still with him.

Chuy said it again, softer this time. In a moment, his anger passed. All that remained was the cracked nail and the blood and dirt clotting on his finger. The wound needed to be cleaned. He staggered to his feet and turned toward the house. From far down the valley came thunder, rolling back and forth between the mountains to the east and the mesa to the west. The monsoons were not over. Chuy raised his face to the sky. He squinted at the high empty blue and could smell the rain in his mind.

The Freedom Pig

When he saw the white man approaching him on horseback, it took all his nerve to stay on the road. He wanted to bolt across the shallow field to his right, dive into a clump of trees he'd noticed across it, and hope there was a way out on the other side. But that would tell the white man his business, and he would lose the pig. So he kept his head down and used the stick he carried to give the pig another tap on the rump. The big pale hog grunted. Their steady trot was a little faster than a long-legged man could comfortably walk.

The white man stopped his horse as they approached, in the shade under some trees along a bend in the road. He was tall and lean, with reddish hair and a broad-rimmed hat. His face was flush from the heat and the ride. The slave slowed to a walk, then stopped beside the big horse. The pig went a few steps further, found a patch of shade at the road's edge, and flopped down in the dust.

The slave kept his head down. He felt the white man's eyes burning on his scalp.

"Where are you taking that pig?"

The voice was deep and forceful.

"Takin' this pig back home, suh. This here is the massa's bes' pig. Got lose this mo'nin'. Foun' him li'l ways back this road, suh."

He kept still and waited. The horse put its head down and exhaled into the dust near the slave's bare feet. The dust felt cool when it settled on his skin. Saddle leather creaked when the white man shifted his weight. The slave looked at the white man's glistening black boot.

"Where do you live?"

The slave pointed up the road.

"'Bout a mile, suh. The Dillard place. Do you know it, suh? Big white house, been there many years."

He heard the saddle creak again and saw the toe of the black boot turn outward. He knew the white man was twisting around to look over his shoulder, back from where he had ridden, back where the slave had pointed. A breeze came up and blew more dust around. The saddle creaked again when the rider resumed his seat. The slave watched the toe of the boot turn forward in the stirrup. He saw that dust had settled on the polished black leather and clouded it.

"The pig got loose?"

"Yassuh. One a th' chilrens lets him loose. The massa hisself gave that youngun a sound beatin'."

There was a brief silence. There was no movement of the air, and no animals or insects passed by or called out. The slave could feel his heart hammering in his chest.

"What's your name?"

"Joseph, suh."

The horse snuffled in the dust again, took a short step forward, and again the saddle leather creaked. Another breeze came by and blew up more dust. The white man coughed. The horse shook his mane and the white man coughed again.

"See that you don't lose your master's pig, Joseph."

"No suh, I will not lose this pig. Good day, suh."

The slave went the few steps to where the pig lay and gave it a tap on the rump with his stick. The pig grunted and got to its feet. They took off trotting again, the big pale hog in the lead and the black man trailing after it.

He listened for the horse moving off behind him and did not hear it. He could feel the white man's eyes burning on his back. He did not turn and look because the white man had enough suspicions. When he heard the deep voice calling to the horse, and then heard the horse's hooves clomping on the dried mud below the dust, he allowed himself a tiny smile.

"Move along, pig," he said, and tapped it on the rump again.

The pig grunted.

❖ ❖ ❖

The slave had started out at first light. He woke up abruptly and knew it was time. He was already dressed. He crouched in the dark and ate a large piece of stale cornbread and gulped some water. He put a flint and a fishing line in his pockets, picked up a short rope that was looped at one end, and went outside. He stood and listened. The cocks had not sounded. He heard no human voices or activity.

There was no moon. The eastern stars were gray dots and the eastern sky was a flat grayish purple. It was cool, but there were no clouds and no wind, so he knew the cool would be gone when the sun cleared the horizon. It would be a long hot day.

He went down to the hogs and let himself into the big boar's pen. It grunted and came toward him, smelled his thigh and snuffled against it. He fell on the pig and got the looped rope around its thick neck. The hog squealed so loud he was sure someone would come. But no one came, so he dragged the pig out of its pen and down toward the road.

He took the rope from the pig's neck and it went a few steps away and lay down. He tied the rope around his middle, under his shirt. He found a good stick under a hickory tree. He tapped the pig on the rump and they set off down the road at a steady trot.

He had to look like he went out after the pig, found it, and was returning home. He couldn't carry anything more than the stick in his hand. It was food and water that he wanted to bring but could not. He had no possessions to leave behind. Even the meager things he bore were not legally his. Even his shirt and pants belonged to his master.

He wasn't a Dillard slave and his name wasn't Joseph. His name was Saturn and he belonged to Jeremy Trevant. The Trevant plantation was fourteen miles behind him when he lied to the white man on the big horse. He covered the distance in three and a half hours, but it seemed no more than twenty minutes. The adrenaline coursing in his veins merged each moment with the next and time lost its meaning.

Saturn was a good judge of distance, and he knew how far he had gone and how far there was to go. There was four more miles of road to the river. He would have to leave the road a mile from the Ohio and turn north, then go another two miles through the woods. The path through the woods was rough and they would move slowly then. They would reach the river in no less than an hour and a half. He tapped the pig again.

"Move along, pig."

He thought he would be tired by now, but his legs moved like they belonged to someone else. He glanced down at his bare feet and thought about the white man's gleaming black boots. He wondered if they would be good walking shoes. He knew that different shoes were good for different things, but he had never worn any. He hoped to get some. He had a long way to go and his feet were already sore.

The road went under some trees and the pig grunted and slowed. It wanted to lie in the cool dust. He whacked it on the rump and it squealed. The pig was not happy, but it was holding up.

They passed the Dillard place ten minutes later. He made sure they moved fast over the quarter mile of open road that fronted it. He did not see anyone, but he could not be sure that no one saw him. He looked at the big white house and felt he knew it, but he had never been there before. He wondered if the old slaves he had met were still there and still alive.

❖ ❖ ❖

Saturn met them only once. They came to the Trevant plantation with Master Dillard, a short fat man no one liked. Dillard stopped to see Master Trevant on business, early in September two years prior. The weather had suddenly turned cool and the sky was high and luminous. The clouds seemed to bump up against it and drift into each other.

Saturn was standing in the yard looking at the clouds when he heard the wagon coming up the road. He was wishing for some shoes. He felt the odd sky signaled a cold winter and he did not want to spend it with his frozen feet bundled in shredded rags.

One of the old slaves was driving the wagon. He had a head of bright white puffy hair that looked to Saturn like one of the clouds he had just been watching. The old slave waved to him and he waved back. The fat white man sitting next to the old slave did not gesture, and even from a distance Saturn could tell he was mean.

The wagon rattled into the yard and the white man started yelling orders before they had stopped. He jumped down and started to the house. Saturn didn't notice the second slave till he clambered from the wagon bed. He was tall and broad-shouldered, with gray hair cut close to his scalp.

The slaves were to unload the wagon. Master Dillard was trading rye and tobacco seed for pigs. Dillard and Trevant had done business before but neither were happy with the experience. The two plantations had not bartered in a number of years, but desire for profit had overcome dislike and they decided to try it again.

The gray-haired slave walked next to him while Saturn led the wagon to the seed shed. The slave introduced himself as James and said the driver was called Grimly. They talked some more while Saturn helped them unload the rye seed. Grimly said very little.

James asked Saturn about himself and his family. It turned out that James and Grimly knew his mother when she was a young woman and lived at another plantation. Saturn told them she was still alive and at the Trevant place, but she was not right. She talked to ghosts and didn't recognize her only living child. She called Saturn "Jonah" and thought he was nine years old.

James said he was sorry to hear that. He said that Saturn's mother had been a beautiful young woman and Grimly had been sweet on her. Grimly nodded and flashed the most incongruously beautiful smile, wide and full of joy, but he said nothing.

While they unloaded the wagon, James asked questions about the Trevant place. Saturn answered them fully. He knew the plantation well and was a student of its failures. He told them the soil was depleted, the master's planning was bad, and the overseer was lazy and cruel. He tried to keep his bitterness from pouring out but he could not. Once he saw James give Grimly a solemn look and he grew embarrassed and stopped talking. But James prompted him again and again he could not still his tongue. There was too much to tell and these old men seemed to care. When he was finally through he felt drained.

When Saturn was empty of words, they did not talk till the load was nearly done. Then Grimly noticed that two spokes on the right front wheel were cracked. James commented that was where Master Dillard always sat and the old men laughed. It took Saturn a moment to join them, and when he did his laughter was forced. When the wagon was empty, Grimly went off to the house to tell Master Dillard about the damaged wheel. James and Saturn waited and talked.

James told about the place where he lived. The Dillard plantation was north and west, toward Ohio. Saturn asked how far it was and James said nine miles to the property and fifteen miles to the house. Then James said it was eighteen miles to the river. Saturn knew the Ohio River wasn't far, but when the old slave told him it was on the other side of the Dillard place, that made it seem close.

Saturn asked James what the river was like, and what was on the other side. The old slave looked into his eyes. James' eyes were dark amber with fine yellow striations. Saturn studied those eyes and they became precious to him.

"Dangerous knowledge," James said.

Saturn turned away. He looked toward the road and the fields on the other side. Corn and wheat, not much of either at the end of a dry summer. He shifted his weight from his right foot to his left, then leaned against the empty wagon. They had tied Dillard's horses nearby and one of them stomped a back hoof and shook off a cloud of flies. Saturn watched the flies disperse, then he looked into James' eyes again. James nodded at him.

Grimly came across the yard and told them Master Dillard had cursed him for the broken wheel, then cursed the roads here about, but they were to fix it. They took the wheel off the wagon and repaired it in the yard outside the tool shed.

Grimly was bending over the wheel when James told him that Saturn wanted to know about the river. Grimly looked up at James and James nodded at him once. Grimly frowned at Saturn, stared deep into his eyes, then he nodded back at James.

While they worked, James told Saturn where the best place to swim the river was and how to get there. He made the young man repeat to him what he had said. Then he told Saturn how to find a farm on the other side that was owned by a Quaker man.

The old slaves had been across on business with their master and met the Quaker in the market. The Quaker had seen them before and had prepared what he was going to say. They talked briefly while Master Dillard was off relieving himself. James told him the directions and instructions the Quaker had given them, and made Saturn repeat them. Then he made Saturn repeat everything again, and then twice again.

When James was satisfied that Saturn would remember, he told him about a Dillard slave that swam the Ohio. The slave got caught three-day's walk from the river. Master Dillard hobbled the slave when he was brought back. Chopped off the end of one foot with an axe.

He had just finished this story when Master Dillard came across the yard from the big house to see if the wheel was fixed. He was in even worse humor than when he arrived. He yelled at his slaves and called them names and cuffed Grimly on the shoulder, then he waddled back to the house.

When Dillard was gone, Saturn asked James why the hobbled slave got caught. James didn't answer that question. Then Saturn asked if the hobbled slave would do anything differently if he had another chance. Grimly looked at Saturn, then he looked away. James said that money was what the hobbled slave wanted. You needed money to keep moving.

Money meant food and better clothes, decent clothes that didn't mark you as a runaway.

When Grimly spoke it surprised the other men. His voice was sour and biting. "A decent-dressed nigger's got a better chance," the old slave said. James watched Grimly. Grimly stared at the hub of the wagon wheel. Saturn frowned and looked back and forth between the two old men.

"How far is it to Canada?" he almost whispered.

The old slaves looked at him.

"We don't know," James said. "But we know it's far."

"Too far for a coupla old men," Grimly added.

They didn't say much after that. A few minutes later the wheel was fixed and Grimly went in the house to tell Master Dillard. While he was gone, James told Saturn a funny story about Grimly's inept courting of Saturn's mother and they laughed away the tension from the preceding subject.

Grimly came back with Masters Dillard and Trevant. James and Saturn followed the white men down to the hog pens and Grimly stayed behind to hitch up the horses. Dillard and Trevant argued over which three of the young pigs Dillard should have, and the short fat man eventually threw up his arms and accepted his hogs under protest.

"You are robbing me, sir," he bellowed. "You know I must be on my way so you take advantage with your terms. You rob me!"

Trevant loudly insisted that Dillard was mistaken. While the two white men argued, Grimly brought the wagon down and James and Saturn got the pigs loaded onto it. Dillard yelled at his slaves again and called them names again, and this time he cuffed

James on the ear. He clambered onto the front seat of the old wagon, which groaned under his weight. Grimly had to shift over on the bench seat to accommodate the white man's bulk. James hopped into the back with the pigs, and they rode off.

Saturn never saw them again.

❖ ❖ ❖

Several times each day, Saturn studied what James had told him, repeated it in his mind the way his crazy mother chanted bible verse. He repeated it again as he and the pig ran past the Dillard mansion. The knowledge was part of him.

His chance to use this knowledge was almost two years coming. Master Trevant took his family to visit a cousin. They left in the morning and would return in three weeks. Saturn hoped to be in Canada by then. The overseer drank when the master was gone, and the night the Trevants left he drank so much he left the women alone.

At midnight Saturn was lying on his cabin's dirt floor listening to the overseer bellow a sea chantey. The overseer was a massive man from Connecticut in his middle forties. He had spent his youth in the whale fleets and on the slave ships. No one knew what he was doing on dry land and everyone but Master Trevant wished he would go back to sea. The Master's wife made no attempt to hide her hatred for the man. He was cruel and dirty and he used the slave women like a devil.

Saturn worked hard the day the Trevants left. He was tired and needed rest but was afraid he would oversleep. He wanted to be off the Trevant property while the dawn was still young and the road still empty. He wanted to get far away while the overseer was still recovering from this night's drink.

His exhausted mind ran over his plan and his preparations and he stared into the dark and worried. Worry always made Saturn angry, and his anger focused on the hollering drunk that wandered among the plantation's clustered buildings. His anger was a sharp clean knife that slit the throat of his worry, that left him calm and confident. The worst that could happen was death. If they didn't give it to him, he could give it to himself.

He fell asleep then, in an instant, and woke an hour later. The overseer was finally silenced, overcome by the whiskey that made him a disturbance in the first place. It was his mother's voice that reached into Saturn's sleep. She kneeled by his side and entreated him.

"Don't go, Jonah," she whispered. "You're such a little boy."

Saturn blinked into the dark. Her face was shadowed. She whispered again.

"Don't go, my darling baby. They will kill you."

He had not told her of his plans and if he had she would not remember. She had read his thoughts before. It still troubled him but he accepted it. She forgot things that had just happened and knew things she should not know. It seemed she was in touch with the other side and he believed that meant she was in some way already dead.

"Don't worry, Momma." His voice was husky, sleep-choked. "I'll be fine."

She crawled to the far corner of the cabin and lay down on the dirt floor. He had learned not to lie to her. If he had denied he was leaving she would have become hysterical. The whites of her eyes glowed at him in the dark. He rolled onto his side, put his back her direction, and fell asleep again. His last waking thoughts were about the overseer and the hell he would catch from Master Trevant for letting Saturn escape. That alone would give worth to whatever he had to endure.

He thought about the overseer again as he and the pig passed the Dillard mansion and entered a grove of trees. The overseer wouldn't be up yet, and when he was up he would move slowly. It could be a few more hours before the overseer knew he was gone. From what the old slaves told him, he guessed it was another hour to where he would cross the Ohio River. He tapped the hog's rump with his hickory stick.

"Keep movin', pig. We're gettin' close."

❖ ❖ ❖

A mile and a half past the Dillard mansion, the road Saturn was on ended at a busier road, a highway, that crossed the river by ferry. Saturn had to travel a half mile of the highway to reach the footpath that led north to the place where he and the pig would swim the river. On the highway he would be very likely to meet other travelers, and his story of returning the pig to the Dillard place would not work. He would be going the wrong direction.

Saturn and the pig ran fast down the half mile of highway and did not meet anyone. Three times Saturn saw motion ahead, a wave of heat or the stir of a tree limb, and mistook it for an approaching wagon or horseman. Three times he almost dragged the pig into the woods, and three times he would've been wrong.

When he found the footpath, Saturn stopped on the side of the road. The pig went a little distance and flopped in the dust. Saturn hiked up his shirt and unwound the rope from his middle. He fell on the pig and got the loop around its thick neck, then he led the pig into the woods.

They went two miles along the footpath, in and out of gullies that drained toward the river. They found a seep at the foot of a hill and drank. The water was cold and left a metallic taste in Saturn's mouth. They crossed another highway, one that followed the river, and a half mile past it they found the little clearing that faced across a slow stretch of the Ohio.

The river was busy. Boats went up it and boats went down. It wasn't as wide as he pictured and it moved faster than he hoped. The dry weather had lowered and dirtied the water. It was muddy and dark.

He tethered the pig to a tree. The pig lay down in the shade, grunted a few times, and slept. It appeared he would have to wait till dark to cross. He had hoped that wouldn't be so, but he was ready for it.

He dug up some grubs and worms. He found a long stick for a pole, tied his fishing line to it, and went out on the riverbank. At first his hands shook standing there for anyone to see, but he grew used to it and his calm returned.

He got his hook out in the water and sat on the ground. He looked at the far bank and his heart flipped over when he realized that was free soil. He had doubted he would make it this far. He carried a picture of himself in his mind, hung by his own hand, swinging by the pig's rope from a twisted old oak. Stealing his own life from his master seemed better than letting him have it. Now maybe this life would be his.

His mind searched for what to worry over. He knew that by now his absence from the Trevant plantation would have been noticed. But it could have taken some time, perhaps till midday. Saturn thought about the overseer and wondered if he was even awake yet. Once the overseer decided Saturn was a runaway, he had an eight-mile ride in the other direction, away from the river, to the nearest town, while still sick from the drink. He would not make good time. Because of his hangover, and since he would leave the plantation unattended if he went, he might send a slave instead, and none of the Trevant slaves would hurry. It would be well after dark, maybe midnight, before the slave catchers and their hounds could get as far as Saturn was now, on the banks of the Ohio River. It would more likely be sometime early tomorrow.

Saturn knew all this before he set out. It was something he had planned on. But he went over it again anyway. Then he thought of the horseman he had passed and wondered if he should worry about him. The white man's suspicions could have grown. He could have stopped at the Trevant place to mention the slave and the pig he had passed on the road. He could then have offered to assist in the chase, to amend for not stopping Saturn when he had the opportunity. But Saturn's gut told him the horseman had other concerns. He seemed a man occupied with his destination.

Saturn thought about the horseman's boots again. He wanted boots like those, shiny and black with thick soles. If those boots were only good for riding that was reason enough to get a horse. He let himself laugh, sitting there on the banks of the Ohio River, looking across it at the free soil on the other side, wanting a horse to justify pretty boots.

His thoughts stayed good and the fish started to bite. He caught three bass, gutted them with a sharp stick and fed the guts to the pig. He used his flint to start a small fire. He cooked the fish and let them cool while he put the fire out. He didn't want the smoke to draw attention. He ate two of the fish and most the third and fed the rest to the pig. He took his line off the stick, coiled it again and put it back in his pocket.

He brought the fishing line because of a bible lesson. The Sunday before the Trevant family left to go visiting, the preacher read about Jesus and the fishermen. "Teach a man to fish," the preacher said, and Saturn realized he could carry a line in his pocket. It bothered him he hadn't thought of that before.

He slept after he ate, back in the trees with the pig. He hadn't meant to and he hadn't occurred to him that he would.

❖ ❖ ❖

When he awoke it was late afternoon. He lay on his back and blinked up through the trees. A lone cloud blotted out the sun and a little chill clutched at his heart when he remembered where he was.

He got to his feet and went to the riverbank. The water was empty. He scanned it and listened. A slight wind disturbed the leaves over his head. The drone of insects was all around. A crow clacked at some distance behind him, then the drumming of a woodpecker came from across the river. He kept his head moving back and forth, looking upriver then down. No sign of man, on the water or off.

Saturn rousted the pig and led it down to the river's edge, then into the dark water. The pig squealed until it almost drowned, then it swam pretty well. Saturn swam breaststroke with the pig's rope in one hand. He had once planned to tie it to his wrist, but it occurred to him that the pig might sink if it drowned, and a sinking pig could drag him under and drown him too.

The water was warm and greasy and his clothes clung to him. His limbs felt leaden. He blinked hard and brought the far bank into focus. It looked further away than it had from up on the bank. A little trickle of fear came up from his belly and his limbs were no longer heavy. He made his breathing and his strokes smooth and even. The pig swam steadily and the rope between them was slack.

For most the way across, they had the river to themselves. He had judged the current right and it carried them at the correct angle. Saturn knew this was true, but the far bank did not seem any closer. The trickle of fear started in his belly again. He blinked hard a second time, and the trees ahead suddenly appeared larger and richer in detail. A few moments of calm followed. His arms and legs felt strong again. Saturn glanced back and guessed that he and the pig were two-thirds of the way across.

Then voices came over the water. Saturn looked upriver and saw a boat. *Keep moving, pig,* he wanted to yell. The voices grew louder.

"Where you goin', nigger?" came booming at him.

Laughter followed, then words he couldn't make out. The same big voice boomed out again:

"He's swimmin' to the promised land with a side a bacon."

More laughter, raucous this time. The audience for the big voice liked that joke. Saturn waited for gunshots that didn't come. The voices continued, but not loud enough for him to hear. The voices were behind him when he and the pig scrambled out of the water. He slipped and went down on his right knee and came up with mud coating his pant leg to his ankle.

"You gonna eat that hog or ride it?" the big voice said.

Saturn didn't look back. He never saw the man that taunted him. He ran for the cover of the woods and dragged the staggering pig behind him.

❖ ❖ ❖

Saturn raised the pig from a little squealer. Master Trevant picked it from the litter and told Saturn that this pig was to get special care. The master had an eye for livestock and he was known for his pigs. Trevant pigs were big and healthy and well-tempered, even gentle. They were agreeable pigs.

The pig grew fast and lived a good life. It ate the best slops, grunted them down greedily, and mounted the sows, who all favored him. He was the golden boar of the Trevant manor.

And Saturn was its slave. He hauled its slops and kept it clean and watched it copulate. Some nights the slops looked better than his own dinner and the girls on the Trevant place where all spoken for by white men. The girl Saturn wanted most didn't care to be touched by a man again for the rest of her days. She was twenty years old and done with life. Saturn understood her feelings and felt all the worse for still wanting her.

A neighboring planter brought a sow over once, to be impregnated by Trevant's prize boar. Saturn listened to the sow's owner talk with Master Trevant. They watched the boar mount the sow and discussed his virtues.

"If you lived nearer a town, sir," the neighbor said, "you could make a handsome bit from that boar's services."

Master Trevant grinned and nodded. He stuck his thumbs in his armpits and rocked back on his heels.

"I could indeed, sir," he said. "That pig is money."

Saturn stopped listening to what the white men said. He stared at the boar servicing the sow. In his mind he saw the hobbled Dillard slave that James had told him about, a man he had never met and never would. He pictured the slave as slender, light-skinned, and bearded, with fine features and a sad tranquil expression. He looked like a Negro Jesus. Saturn saw the hobbled slave's lips move and heard a deep voice say *money*.

❖ ❖ ❖

The arid heat dried his clothes. The mud caked on his pants became stiff. He stopped the pig and broke up the mud with his hands, then rubbed his hands together to rid them of the dirt.

Saturn knew they were about a mile from the river and had another three miles to the Quaker's farm. Soon they would leave the footpath and take a back road through the woods. He wanted to move fast over this road and decided to rest a bit first. The pig was irritable and tired and balked frequently. He hoped a little rest would improve its traveling mood.

He sat on a log and the pig flopped down at his feet, its belly towards him. He rubbed the hog's belly with his foot, and the animal grunted and sighed and fell asleep. Saturn let the pig sleep for about fifteen minutes. Then he rousted it up and the pig was better behaved. They found the road a hundred yards further on, over a slight rise, and trotted along at the same good pace they had kept most the morning.

Saturn was grateful then for this good pig. He wondered what he would have done if it was not so agreeable and he thanked God for it. He wondered if God had sent him this special hog to take him to freedom. He looked at the pig with respect then, and let it set their pace along the back road. It kept up its trot without prompting from Saturn. He had no need of the hickory stick he had left behind in Virginia. The rope around the pig's neck was slack in Saturn's hand.

The evening was quiet and the heat had broken. The muted voices of birds and bugs merged in a low drowsy hum. They went two miles down the road with the shuffle and clomp of their feet and hooves the loudest sounds they could hear.

Then came the sound of horses behind them, and the rattle of a wagon. It was coming upon them fast. Saturn pulled the rope tight and dragged the pig into the woods. The pig did not complain. Saturn ducked behind an oak and pushed the pig down at his feet. He turned to watch a patch of the road between the tree trunks. The sound of the wagon came and roared past, but all he saw was a gray transparent blur, like a wave of thick heat rushing through the dusty air. No horses, no men, no wagon. Goose bumps went down his arms.

Saturn and the pig crept back to the road and Saturn looked at the dust. He saw only his own footprints and the marks from the pig's hooves. No horse's hooves and no wagon wheels. He looked down the road ahead of him, the way the wagon had gone, and saw that gray transparent blur again in his mind's eye.

He looked down at the pig. It was standing by his side, looking calm, even thoughtful. Saturn felt soothed by the pig and safe with it. They set off down the road again.

❖ ❖ ❖

The farmhouse was a quarter mile from the road, at the edge of twenty cleared acres. It was a small two-story house of wood planks painted white. Saturn stood in the front yard and called hello. He saw a woman's face in a downstairs window, then a man's voice answered from behind the house. He walked around toward it. His knees shook and the pig's hooves fell heavily on the dirt.

A stout white man stood in the backyard. He wore dark somber clothing and squinted at Saturn and the pig. He had an axe in his hands. Saturn stared at the axe.

"Who sent you?" the Quaker said. He had an accent.

"The Dillard slaves."

"What's their names, then?"

"Hamlet and Ulysses."

"Which is which?"

"Grimly is Hamlet and James is Ulysses."

The Quaker had concocted these pseudonyms as passwords and told them to the Dillard slaves during their one brief conversation four years prior at the local market. Saturn was the second runaway to use them. The first was finishing his life with half a foot back at the Dillard place.

The Quaker nodded and put the axe down.

"Nice pig. Come along."

He led them to a small barn at the back of the yard. They went in through the open doors and he pointed into the hayloft.

"Climb up there and stay put. You hear anyone coming, get under that hay. I'll hide the pig. When it's dark, I'll come get you."

Saturn nodded, handed the pig's rope to the Quaker, and started up the ladder.

He slept again in the hayloft, and again it surprised him. He dreamt of the swim across the river and this time the pig and he both drowned. The boat that passed went over them and he could hear the men aboard it laughing.

It was dusk when he woke and the hayloft was dark. He didn't know where he was. He moved and the hay crackled loudly and the sound froze his heart. He didn't breathe for a long moment, until he saw stars and spangles at the edges of his vision.

The Quaker came for him an hour later. He heard heavy boot steps outside and knew it was time to go. He waited till the white man called him down, then he scrambled out of the hayloft. They stood next to each other in the open barn doors. The Quaker handed him a small bundle tied in dark cloth.

"Some food," he said.

In his other hand was a tin pitcher and cup. He held them up so Saturn could see.

"And water. You can drink now, but I'll have to ask you to eat your meal away from here."

He poured a cup and handed it to Saturn. The water was cool and clear. Saturn drained the cup and the Quaker refilled it. Saturn emptied the cup five times.

"Do you want to sell the pig?"

Saturn nodded. The Quaker took a small sack of coins from a vest pocket.

"That's a fair price. You might have done better at market, but I cannot spare more. I wish that I could."

Saturn took the coins and clutched it in his fist. The Quaker put his hands on his hips.

"There is nowhere next to send you. There was another man north of here, but he died and his family returned east."

Saturn didn't know what the Quaker was talking about. He had been told only of this farm and this man, a single known stop on the long journey north. Beyond here, he expected nothing, no help he didn't buy.

The Quaker squinted at him.

"Do you know which way is north, then?"

Saturn hesitated, then pointed to his right and a little ahead. The Quaker nodded.

"Maybe you'll be alright, then."

He took a piece of paper from his shirt pocket and unfolded it. He held it so they both could see and they turned together so it caught the moonlight.

"A map. It will take you about ten miles north. Can you read it?"

"Not the writing."

"Can you make sense of the pictures, then?"

The Quaker pointed at a winding line.

"There's a stream you can follow."

He pointed at two straight lines that crossed the winding one.

"There's a bridge over the stream. You see that, then?"

Saturn nodded at the paper. The Quaker pointed at a small rectangle with a cross next to it, near the top of the map.

"This is a church. Unitarians. They may help you."

Saturn nodded again. The Quaker folded the map and held it out for Saturn to take. Saturn put the sack of coins in the pants pocket that held his flint. He took the map and held it in his hand.

"Thank you."

"Thank the Lord, son. I only do his work."

A thin cloud slipped over the moon and the farmyard darkened. Saturn looked at the Quaker and wished he could see him better.

"Thank you just the same."

"Well, you're welcome then, and God bless you."

They did not talk for a long quiet moment. Saturn slipped the map into the pocket that held his money and his flint, then he pointed past the house, toward the drive out front.

"Back on the road a ways, I thought I heard a wagon."

"But there wasn't any wagon."

"No."

The Quaker put his hands back on his hips.

"One of our first nights on this farm, it rode right into our front yard. Woke us all up, my wife and daughters and myself. We went outside and looked for it. I couldn't see a thing, but my oldest girl said she saw something moving in the darkness. I had my rifle and I pointed it in the direction she showed me. I yelled, 'who is it?' but there was no answer. Then it started off again. My wife and the girls ran inside and I waved my rifle around like a fool. I went inside when I couldn't hear anything more. My oldest girl said she could still hear it, faintly, riding away from us."

A shiver went down Saturn's neck and shoulders. He did not want to share the road with a ghost wagon.

"Does it ride by here often?"

"We've heard it thrice in two years. My wife heard it this evening, after it passed you."

Saturn felt better. His mother, who knew about ghosts, said they kept strict habits. If the wagon had been an infrequent visitor, he was not likely to see it again. He felt better still when thc cloud passed and the moon re-lit the farmyard. But he jumped slightly when the Quaker put a hand on his shoulder.

"You best be off, lad. You are a danger to us all."

The Quaker turned and left, moved quickly across the yard and into the shadow of the house. His dark clothes made him invisible then. Saturn saw the edge of a white door when it came out into the moonlight, then the door was gone and he heard it slam.

He walked around the house and up the dirt drive. There was a clearing not far from the house. He stopped in the pool of moonlight, set his bundle of food on the ground, and tried to count his money. There were coins he didn't recognize, and he guessed correctly that they were worth more than the ones he knew. He counted the coins he was familiar with and that was more than all the money he had held in his entire life. *That pig is money*, he thought, and he laughed quietly.

He turned around and looked back toward the house. There was a bend in the drive and all he could see was one corner of white planks. He missed the pig and wished he could keep it. The thought of traveling alone made the pit of his stomach drop. He wanted to go back and see the pig one last time, rub its belly and hear it grunt. But he didn't want to bother the Quaker man or his family.

"Goodbye, pig," he said, in a quiet voice.

Now all he had to do was find Canada.

❖ ❖ ❖

When Jeremy Trevant brought his family home and found his best pig gone and one of his best slaves with it, he loaded his long gun, pointed it at the overseer, and ordered him off the property. There was an argument and the overseer charged Trevant, who shot him in the leg.

The doctor was sent for and arrived the next morning. He was back again in a week, found gangrene had set in, and took off the leg. When the operation was finished, the overseer rose up off the table, gave an enormous roar, and died. Trevant's wife refused him burial in the family graveyard. So he was laid to rest in the slave graveyard, with a rough cross of wood that soon disappeared.

The Trevant plantation was in decline when Saturn escaped. Five years later, under Master Trevant's sole hand after the death of the overseer, conditions were bad enough to send Mrs. Trevant home to Kentucky. She took their children with her. Master Trevant slowly sold off his slaves and parcels of land. As an old man, he fell from his horse and died. The remaining property passed to his oldest son, who was busy with other matters. When Union Cavalry rode through during the war, they found the big house empty and only a very old and crazy black woman living by herself in a tumbledown shack.

When Master Trevant returned from visiting his cousin and shot his overseer, Saturn was not in Canada as he had hoped. He was still in Ohio, in the northeast corner of the state near Lake Erie and Pennsylvania, hidden by a Unitarian family on another small farm. Three weeks later Saturn left the United States at Niagara Falls. He went to work on a farm in Ontario and proved himself adept with the livestock, especially the pigs. He saved his wages and bought himself a pair of shiny black boots that he wore on Sundays to service.

For the rest of his life, Saturn had a reoccurring dream. He would ride into the Trevant plantation on the back of big black horse, dressed in good riding clothes with glistening black thick-soled boots. He would find his mother outside her cabin and dismount to embrace her. She would place a hand on his cheek and call him *Jonah*. In the mornings after this dream, Saturn often wondered what became of the pig that crossed the Ohio River and bought his freedom.

The pig never left the Quaker's farm. The Quaker and his family liked the pig and treated it well. The big boar went back to his old life, eating rich slops and mounting sows. The Quaker sold the boar's services and his progeny filled the neighboring farms. He lived a long happy life and was buried like a family member when his time had passed.

About the Author

Al Sim was born in Michigan and lived there till he was six. He spent the rest of his childhood and early adulthood in Pennsylvania, with the exception of eleven months on Wake Island in the North Pacific. He graduated *magna cum laude* from New York University with a degree in economics.

During and after college, Sim has lived in Manhattan and Brooklyn, in central Massachusetts and on Cape Cod, and in New Mexico, Virginia, and Arizona. He has worked in restaurants, in factories and warehouses, on construction sites, and on Wall Street. He is currently employed in the software industry. He is married and has two children. Their domestic life is monitored by two cats.

Sim's fiction has appeared in numerous publications; credits appear on the copyright page at the beginning of this book. He is working on a second volume of stories, set in the fictional village of Los Huertos (included in this collection are "Chuy's Truck," "No Mix," and "La Estupidez de Cosas").

Cover Artist

Geoffrey Atkin is a New York-based artist who specializes in oil and pastel portraits and interiors. He says of his work, "I've always been fascinated by the emotional and philosophical qualities of light, and have been captivated since youth by the works of Vermeer and Velazquez.

"My main source of formal training came from the High School of Music and Art (1982–86). Rather than art school, I decided to attend Williams, a liberal arts college. However, I've learned so much since at The Painting Group, an art class founded and taught by David Levine and Aaron Shikler, which meets every Wednesday on Green Street in Soho. I've been attending for twelve years now. Working in the class on a regular basis has helped me refine my abilities to render the figure through drawing and painting from a live model, as well as giving me exposure to painters who share my aesthetic sense. And attending a liberal arts college helped both broaden and deepen my conceptual range.

"I took three trips to Italy—in 1989, '93, and '95—and I believe these experiences affected my early development more than anything else, chiefly through being exposed to Rome: its light, its history, and of course, its art. Since then, the most important development in my life has certainly been the births of my three wonderful sons. Much of my current work is about the wonders and perils of childhood and growing up."

Geoffrey is currently a member of Atlantic Gallery, in Soho in Manhattan. Learn more about Geoffrey and his art at www.gcagallery.com.

A Note on the Type

~

The text of this book is set in Bookman Old Style, designed by Alexander Phemister, a punchcutter at Miller & Richard foundry in Edinburgh, Scotland, in the 1850s. Phemister ended his career at the Dickson foundry in Boston, Massachusetts, where he became a partner and continued designing type until he retired in 1891. Alexander Phemister was born in Edinburgh, Scotland, in 1829 and died in Boston, Massachusetts, in 1894.

Praise for Al Sim

~Continued from back cover~

Sim's sense of place is so strong and physical, the reader feels like he's watching from behind a bush, waiting to see what happens.

—Linda Swanson-Davies, Co-Editor,
Glimmer Train Stories

In "Two Head Gone," Sim illuminates the plight of Harold Rhinebeck, an amateur who has to reconcile himself to his own mediocrity, and a desperate situation. The story reflects a knowing familiarity with the landscape of human fallibility. That the portrayal also evokes such sympathy from the reader is testament to Sim's honesty and grace as a writer.

—Harris Levinson, Co-Editor,
Crab Creek Review

Al Sim creates characters that live and breathe, taking readers along on a journey that reveals the complex internal and external world of the "average man." In "Chuy's Truck," Sim offers equal measures of humor and the bittersweet, giving us a memorable visit with a charming, if laconic, character.

—Pam McCully, Editor,
Lynx Eye

"Nick the Greek" won me by its honesty, its quirky tone—ironic detachment yielding to heartfelt truth. Al Sim committed this story to paper with integrity born of a resolve to express important truths about the human heart.

—Don Williams, Founding Editor,
New Millennium Writings

In "Last Round Joey Two Bits," Al Sim takes the reader through all the stereotypes you expect to encounter in a story about a washed-up boxer who refused to take a fall. And with Mobius-strip like perfection, Sim brings you around again, exactly where you began, with a deeper respect, even affection, not only for the boxer and his Wise-Guy pals, but for the lives that built these stereotypes—and transcend them.

—Dr. Carman C. Curton, Faculty Advisor,
Talking River Review

Al Sim creates his own peculiar, yet utterly engaging and believable world. People—not characters—interact in a way that is at once wry and disturbing. "La Estupidez de Cosas" has an insidious sense of threat pervading the narrative.

—Gregor Milne, Editor,
Projected Letters

Al Sim's "The Bully Bleeder" is an original take on coming of age. In an apartment complex peopled with kids from broken families, an anti-hero and an anti-villain vie for control of a group of boys. Not your typical good guy-bad guy tale, Sim's characterization captures the vulnerability of childhood wrapped in a toughened exterior. As the narrator recounts, in Sim's authentic voice of a teenager, recalling an incident where the title character experiences a reversal of power, the reader rediscovers the meaning of the old adage: no one can control you without your permission. "The Bully Bleeder" is a fresh and exciting read from the imagination of a talented writer.

—Rebekah Anderson, Managing Editor,
Washington Square Review

First published in *Chiricú*, the Chicano-Riqueño Studies Literary Journal at Indiana University, Al Sim's "No Mix" demonstrates how cultural and racial differences are profoundly affected by the real economic disparities of his characters. By subverting its own categories, Sim's narrative escapes its own constraints and cleverly breaks away from the inherent inclination to adhere to essentialist categories. In this respect, his story initiates a timely discussion about cultural relations in the United States, while offering a critique of problematic assumptions that we find ourselves compelled to make.

—Roberto Vela Córdova, Assistant Professor,
Department of Language and Literature,
Texas A & M University

Printed in the United States
43091LVS00003B/364-411